Lock Down Publications and Ca$h
Presents

I0680368

CORNER BOY
Destined To Rise

Written By
COREY ROBINSON

First Edition 2024

Printed in the United States of America

This is a work of fiction. Names, characters, places, and incidents either
are products of the author's imagination or are used fictitiously. Any
similarity to actual events or locales or persons, living or dead, is
entirely coincidental.

Lock Down Publications
P.O. Box 944
Stockbridge, GA 30281
www.lockdownpublications.com

Like our page on Facebook: Lock Down Publications
www.facebook.com/lockdownpublications.ldp

Stay Connected with Us!

Text **LOCKDOWN** to 22828 to stay up-to-date with new releases, sneak peaks, contests and more…

Like our page on Facebook:
Lock Down Publications

Join Lock Down Publications/The New Era Reading Group

Visit our website:
www.lockdownpublications.com

Follow us on Instagram:
Lock Down Publications

Email Us: We want to hear from you!

Chapter 1

"Nigga, why I always catch you watchin' that cracka? You trying to get your dick sucked or something?"

"Fuck you, D. I ain't trying to get shit. I just find her interesting, that's all."

"Interesting? The fuck is so interesting about a white bitch on that pipe? Damn, Jamir, all these fine ass sistas in the neighborhood and you sitting here sweating her pale ass. What the hell is wrong with you?"

"Ain't shit wrong, nigga, and ain't nobody sweating a damn thing. Your ass just trippin' and shit. You know what? It's getting late and my black ass is getting tired, so I'ma get up outta here. I'll catch up with you later."

"A'ight yo. I should probably get out of here, too. Trish ass been on that bullshit lately. She swears I'm out here slanging dick instead of rocks."

"Oh yea? Well, don't worry, Danny boy, I ain't gonna tell her that she's right. Your secret is safe with me."

Jamir had known Danny since their sandbox days, but for some reason, he just couldn't bring himself to fully trust him. He had never been the type of nigga to be on that super friendly shit, because he felt like the last thing he needed in his life was a co-defendant. He knew how niggas got down when the heat was on. He also knew that when a beef came, they would run like pussies. At one time, there was a code that people in the streets lived by, but that shit had changed. Jamir felt like most of the niggas that hung in the hood were

4

straight bitches. Mufuckas would walk around and scream about how real they were, when in all actuality, they were really rats. Jamir wasn't like that, though. He swore that he would never sell his soul because he considered himself a real trap nigga.

Jamir had decided at a young age that he was going to sell dope and hit licks for a living. He knew what he wanted to be from the time he could hold his own dick and piss in a grown folk's toilet. The thought of having a real job never crossed his mind. He knew that those bullshit ass paychecks wouldn't be enough to move a damn thing. Jamir wanted better than he was used to, and he knew in order to make that happen, he would have to do shit on his own.

He had grown up as a dirty ass little ghetto kid and was accustomed to getting out of bed in the mornings and stepping over empty crack vials. His pops had been on that shit ever since he could remember. No matter how hard his momma tried, she just couldn't convince him to leave it alone. When she finally found the strength to walk away, she took Jamir and his little sister, Missy, to live with their grandmother, while she went in another direction. Word on the street was that she'd had another man on the side all along. That man welcomed her with open arms but told her she would have to leave her two little crumb snatchers behind. He didn't want children, especially ones that belonged to another man. It took years for Jamir and his sister to get over it, but they eventually pushed their mother out of their minds and never looked back.

Unfortunately, their grandmother made them go to church every Sunday. Missy loved getting all dressed up, but Jamir hated everything about it. He couldn't stand to sit on those hard ass benches for hours while the old women screamed and shouted for the Lord to wash all their sins away, even though they would turn around and sin again.

One Sunday morning, while Jamir's mind was going one hundred miles an hour, he noticed the pastor pick up the collection plate and pass it to the usher. Jamir was old enough to understand that nothing in the world moved without money, so while the rest of the congregation was focused on praising the almighty, he kept his eyes on that plate. He wondered what the church would be doing with all the money they collected because it seemed to him that they already had everything they needed. If not, he was sure the God they served would provide the rest.

Jamir sat back and watched as old Ms. Garvey pulled a fifty-dollar bill from her oversized breasts and then dropped it in the plate with the ones and fives that were already there. He wondered what else she had hidden down there, but brushed the thought away once that plate of money made it to his hands. When it did, he reached in and pulled that fifty back out and slid it into his pocket. As far as he could tell, no one had seen him commit the sin, so he didn't feel the need to repent and ask for forgiveness. Jamir needed that money and much more, so that he could fulfill his future dreams. He knew that for a mufucka to understand his get down, they would first have to understand his come up.

While other boys his age had been plotting ways to cop name brands, Jamir was laid back thinking up game plans. That being broke shit was not part of his agenda, and he knew that if he wanted to change things, he would have to get out there and make a play. When he was growing up, he never really had nice shit because his pops smoked up most of the funds that came through the front door. Jamir was determined to make it on his own, by any means necessary.

Jamir ended up stashing away all the money he had taken out of the collection plate until he had accumulated enough to buy his first package. It wasn't a major purchase, but it was enough to get him started on his journey. He had always known that he was destined to be a drug dealer, and at fifteen, he deemed himself an official corner boy. Jamir hit the block and ran. He refused to let anyone stop him. He ran so fast that he eventually worked himself up to a key.

A lot of the older niggas on the block tried to recruit him to work for them, but Jamir wasn't willing to kiss ass just to be bigger and better. He knew that he was destined to rise, and that after some time, his light would shine on its own, so he kept on thuggin'. He was just getting started, but because of his hunger and determination, he rose quickly up the chain. Jamir wasn't exactly where he wanted to be, but at eighteen, he had become the nigga to see.

Jamir lit his wineberry Black & Mild and pulled away from the block. He always made sure to ride dolo because he didn't trust other mufuckas up in his shit. He had been too afraid that some sucka would plant something on him, and thanks to his paranoia, he had managed to stay free and alive. He knew niggas claimed all the time that money wasn't everything, but then would turn around and kill a mufucka for it. That was one of the main reasons Jamir never tried to upstage the next man. He felt that if he leveled up too high and too quick, it would cause jealousy and bring him unwanted drama. He also didn't want or need any extra attention from the boys in blue. Those crackers hated to see a young black man on his grind. So far, Jamir had managed to stay off their radar, and he planned to keep it that way.

It was late, but it was also the first of the month. The fiends were out and about trying to spend their last few dollars before calling it a night. Unlike some of the other dealers, Jamir didn't mind breaking off hits for a few dollars. He believed that no matter the amount, every single penny counted, and he wasn't about to let any of it slip by. He noticed Mary, a forty-something year old smoker that stayed pregnant, who was also his pop's sister. He could only shake his head when she spotted him and tried to wave him down. She had tried time after time to throw him the pussy. She didn't care that he was her nephew, as long as she got what she wanted, but Jamir didn't trick off his stash like the others did. There was only one person he was willing to share a piece of the rock with, and he was determined to do just that.

Rachel was the only white girl who could walk around the hood like she owned it. She had been hanging around the west end for years, and the niggas seemed to like having her around, especially old man Nate. He owned a small store in the neighborhood where you could walk in and buy single cigarettes for a quarter. That worked out perfect for the crackheads because most of the time, small change was all they had in their pockets. Rachel could go in that store anytime she wanted and walk out with whatever she desired. Word was, that when she went in there, she'd give Nate a quick head job in the bathroom located in the back of the store in exchange for some cash. The rumors had never proven to be true but somehow, they were still believed.

Bitches around the way knew not to fuck with Rachel, no matter how much time she spent with their niggas. It somehow became an unwritten rule, and it was well respected.

Rachel may have been an eighteen-year-old crackhead, but you could never look at her and tell it. She stayed clean and in fresh gear. She even kept her hair and makeup done. She was also thick in all the right places, and not even hitting the pipe could change that. There was just something about her that intrigued Jamir, but he didn't want anyone else to know it. He was on a mission to rise up and be somebody in the game. The last thing he needed was for the other niggas to find out he was feeling a smoker. It would ruin his reputation for sure and possibly weaken his status in the streets. He wasn't willing to set his pride to the side and let anything jeopardize his climb.

It was late. Jamir still had a few rocks left in his pocket and he didn't want to go home alone. He had been staying in his great-grandfather's house ever since the old man had been put in a convalescent home. It was nice not having any rent to pay, but it got really lonely at night. His younger sister, Missy, had asked him to let her move in, but Jamir liked his privacy, and he knew that Missy talked too much.

He didn't want his business getting out there like that, so he had to turn his sister down.

Jamir made sure to look around real good. He had to be certain that no one was watching him. Once he was satisfied that only God's eyes were on him, he pulled up beside the object of his desire. As soon as he rolled the window down on his used Buick, he could smell her sweet, fruity scent, and it caused his dick to rock up instantly. He quietly wondered just how many niggas she had been with that night, but he didn't want to dwell on it, so he pushed it out of his mind.

"Sup, Rachel? You feel like chillin' with me for a little while? A nigga got a little something left in his pocket just for you. What do you say?"

She smiled at the thought of getting with Jamir. She had seen him serving on the block, but he never seemed to pay her any attention, unlike other female smokers. She had never lost her dignity, so she never could bring herself to beg for dope, especially from a nigga like Jamir. He may not have been the biggest fish in the sea, but to her, he was the best catch. She always thought that he resembled her favorite rapper, Ludacris, and anytime she would hear one of Luda's raps, she would smile and think of Jamir.

"Yeah, I guess I could hang out for a while. There's nothing going on out here anyway. But just so you know, I like to take me a hit first."

"You straight. Shit, I got my own thang going on, so you can have whatever I got left."

Rachel thought about it for a minute and then shrugged her shoulders before getting into the passenger side of his ride, a place she couldn't ever remember seeing another female. She was about to ask him if he had a girlfriend but thought better of it. He didn't pick her up to answer questions that she had no place asking, so she would respect his mind. She figured that anything he wanted her to know, he would tell her on his own, so she stayed quiet and listened as Toosii pumped out of the speakers.

She thought that Jamir would have driven something a little more plush, but she didn't dwell on it. She figured he just preferred to be low key, instead of flashy, like the others. When he pulled up in the driveway of a small wooden house, she raised her brows because even it wasn't top notch. However, his material things were of no concern to her, as long as he gave her what she had come there for. She was even more thrown off when he took her inside. The house was furnished with items that looked like they came from a different era, a much older one. She wondered why he hadn't at least updated the place but figured that maybe he just liked it the way it was.

"Why don't you go on in the bathroom and run some bath water, wash up and make that pussy fresh for me."

"Um, okay, but when you gonna let me take a hit? I like to get mine up front."

"Don't worry, I'll have your shit ready as soon as you get cleaned up. You're in good hands with me. Now go ahead and handle that. I don't like to go in behind the next nigga. I'ma take some chances with you though, as long as you keep it between us. I don't like other mufuckas in my business. You understand?"

"You have nothing to worry about because I don't tell my business. I'm sure that everybody feels like they know everything about me, but they don't. I can assure you that I don't do half the stuff they think I do."

After she said it, she began to strip out of her clothes right in front of Jamir. She wanted him to see what she had in store for him. She knew her body was right because she took very good care of it. She watched him look at her perky breasts and then down to her pussy. When she turned to walk away, she could feel his eyes on her backside, so she made sure to sway a little harder. Jamir had to admit that he liked what he saw and couldn't wait to have her on his dick. He could already see himself grabbing her ass cheeks as he slid in and out of her. He reached down and grabbed his nutsack and

10

squeezed it. The anticipation continued to build, and he was glad that she was in the bathroom because he was a little embarrassed by his anxiousness.

While she freshened up the goods, Jamir decided to take the time to snort a line of the cocaine he had in his pocket. No one on the block knew that he had a habit, and he planned to keep it that way. He wasn't sure why, but he felt more at ease with the white girl and just wanted to enjoy the rest of his night. Jamir took a long sniff of the powder and held his head back so the drug could drain down his nasal cavity to the back of his throat. He closed his eyes and basked in the numb feeling the cocaine left behind. He felt like he had a habit he could break at any time, but cocaine was like a bitch you just couldn't get rid of.

Jamir heard a noise and brought his head down. He opened his eyes only to find Rachel standing in front of him. She noticed the cocaine dust that laid on the small mirror but it didn't seem to faze her. She figured that if cocaine was his thing, who was she to judge? Jamir smiled a one-sided smile at her and then pulled the baggie of rocks from his pocket. He sat it on the dresser beside the mirror he had been using to line up his fix, and then stood.

"Go 'head and do ya thang, ma. It's all yours."

"You got an empty soda-can that I can use?"

Jamir looked at her confused but found what she had asked him for. She took the can and rinsed it out before pushing one side of it in to form a dent. Jamir scrunched his eyebrows together as he watched her take a safety pin and poke small holes in the dent and then she lit a Newport. She dumped the ashes from the cigarette on to the holes until she felt like she had enough. Jamir knew that crackheads had several ways to get their high on, but it was the first time he had seen someone do it that way. He quietly wondered why she didn't have a pipe like other smokers, but he didn't want to ruin the moment and ask her, so he let her be.

She picked up one of the rocks and broke a piece off and then placed the piece carefully on top of the ashes. She then put the aluminum can to her lips. She struck the lighter and brought it up closer to the can, but before she could put the flame to the drug, she locked eyes with Jamir. All of a sudden, Rachel felt guilty and a little less human. He noticed her hesitation and wondered what was wrong.

"Aye, what's up? You good ma? You need help or something?"

"No, um, could you just not watch me? I don't like to be stared at when I'm trying to take a hit. It's a little uncomfortable."

"Oh shit, my bad. I ain't know. I gotta take a piss anyway, so I'ma go handle that and come back. You gonna be done by then?"

Rachel nodded her head and waited for Jamir to leave the room before she struck her lighter again. Up until that moment, she had never been ashamed of what she did. She couldn't understand why she felt that way because Jamir was just a trick like any other nigga. For some reason, though, she wanted him to respect her, but how could he when she had a crack can glued to her mouth? The drug suddenly became less appealing, and she realized that she wouldn't be able to enjoy it as long as he was in her presence. She decided to stash the dope in her shoe and give Jamir what he had paid for. She would take the dope with her and smoke it later when she could truly enjoy it. As soon as he walked back in the room, Rachel crushed the can and threw it away.

"Damn, you smoke all that shit already? Your ass ain't playing with it."

"No, Jamir, I didn't smoke it. I just don't feel like getting high right now. I've suddenly lost the urge, but I'm ready to handle my business with you. Go ahead and get undressed so I can get started."

Jamir shrugged and slid his jeans and boxers down. He stepped out of them, sat on the bed and began to stroke his manhood. He could feel his nuts throb from the anticipation of releasing his seed into her wet ocean, but first, he wanted to feel her mouth on him. He stared deep into her green eyes as the pre-cum formed on the head of his dick. Rachel watched his every move with desire that she never knew she had in her. She raised one eyebrow and smiled.

"Looks like you're ready for a real bitch to do things to you that you've only dreamed of."

"Oh yeah? Question is, can you handle a real nigga like me?"

"Guess you'll find out."

Rachel got up on the bed and bent over him. He watched as she licked the pre-cum off his tip and then slowly made his length disappear between her lips. She sucked his dick like a tootsie pop and caused his toes to curl. He could have sworn that he had died and gone to heaven but then, he second guessed it because not even heaven could make a mufucka feel that good.

Jamir put a hand on the back of her head and grinded his pelvic to meet her slow and steady rhythm. No sooner than he did it, he felt the coolness of the room brush against his flesh. He quickly opened his eyes and saw that Rachel was straddling him. He grunted in pleasure as soon as his dick felt her wetness. Her pussy was tighter than he could have ever imagined. Even though he knew he should have been strapped up, he couldn't bring himself to stop her.

Rachel slid up and down his dick like a professional porn star. Jamir was far from a virgin, but she made him feel like it was his first time. He couldn't even imagine sticking his dick in another pussy after hers. But as bad as he wanted to keep her there forever, he knew that he couldn't. Jamir had come too far to get pussy whipped by a crackhead, but it was too late to turn back. She had blown his mind and the thought of her with another nigga caused him to push her off his dick.

"Turn over and let me hit that pussy from the back."

Rachel did exactly what he told her to do because right at that moment, she would have done anything he asked of her. Jamir's dick was top of the line and taking her to a world she never knew existed. Jamir and Rachel's fuck turned into more than either of them could have imagined. They were on a completely different kind of high and neither one of them wanted to come down.

Morning came quicker than ever, and the sounds of knocking woke Jamir from his deep, sex induced slumber. He opened his eyes and realized that Rachel was still beside him and panicked. He knew that it could only be Danny fucking with him that early and the last thing he needed was for him to find out Rachel had spent the night in his arms. He and Danny were cool, but he didn't want him all in his business like that.

"Yo, Rachel, you gotta get up and get outta here. I can't let my boy know you been up in here all night."

She wouldn't admit it, but his words stung like an angry bee. She knew from the jump that getting with him was too good to be true. She was just a crackhead in his eyes, and that was all she would ever be to him. She wouldn't comment on what he had said, but she needed him to know what they shared meant something to her. Deep down inside, she felt like it had meant something to him too, but she could never get him to admit that. While Jamir rushed to put on his clothes, she took her time. Her wounded heart wouldn't allow her to move any faster, but Jamir was determined to get her out of there in a hurry.

"Come on. The fuck you moving so slow for? I'll catch up with you later and throw you a little something extra, but I can't afford to let anyone know that you stayed here all night. I'd never be able to live that shit up."

"What's the matter, Jamir? You ashamed of falling asleep with a crackhead in your arms?"

"Nah, I ain't ashamed of shit, but I do got a reputation to uphold. Tricking off and sending you on your way is one

14

thing, but letting you stay all night is a whole other issue. Mufuckas might get the wrong impression and think a nigga is catching feelings and shit."

"Is there something wrong with that? I mean, you can't help who you like."

Jamir thought about what she said but he couldn't afford to push his pride to the side and act on what he felt. He didn't want to lose the hood's respect after how hard he had worked to get it. Besides, how far could he actually go with a crackhead by his side? Danny knocked again and brought him back to reality.

"Look, I just need you up outta here, a'ight?"

Rachel had never felt so used. She only got high because it filled a void she had in her life. She would give it all up to be seen as somebody worthy. She looked up at Jamir one last time and then bent down and pulled the package he had given her out of her shoe. She laid it on the dresser and walked out the back door, closing it gently behind her.

Jamir looked at the package and felt like shit. He understood the message behind her leaving it. She had been there only because of him, not for what he possessed and yet, he still chose to play hard. He was too worried about what others would say if they found out. He knew that rising to the top could sometimes bring heartache, but he brushed that shit off and opened the door for Danny.

Chapter 2

While out on the block with Danny, Jamir couldn't shake the thoughts of the night he had with Rachel. He was still trying to process the fact that she gave him his drugs back. He knew that she was different from the other fiends, but he never would have guessed her to do a move like that. He wondered why he hadn't seen her out that night, but he didn't sweat it too hard because the block had been slower than usual.

"Shit been real slow out here tonight. I say we call it and go in early. I'm sure Trish would appreciate having you in before the streets close. What do you say?"

"Fuck that. I don't wanna hear her ass bitchin'. That shit done got old."

"Well, my nigga, don't you think you should have thought of that before you ran up in it raw and planted a seed? You might have been caught up in the moment but that shit got you stuck for eighteen years."

"You don't think I know that? Bruh, I just turned nineteen, and I'm already tied the fuck down. I ain't thrilled about that shit, but I ain't gonna lie, every time I look into DJ's eyes or hold him in my arms, it makes all the bullshit I go through worth it. I'll never regret making that lil nigga. I just wish I would have planted his ass in a different garden."

"Nigga, you shot out. I just hope you learned from your mistakes and keep that mufucka wrapped up. Bitches out here in the hood stay fertile, and they be checking on a daily for a young dealer on they come up. Trying to lock a nigga down and shit. Gotta be cautious out here in these streets. Know what I'm saying?"

"Don't worry, I learned my lesson. I stay strapped up now. Pockets stay full."

Danny reached in his pocket and pulled out a handful of condoms to show Jamir. The two of them shared a laugh and a high-five. Shit was real when the hoes came to holler. Niggas had to do what they could to keep from getting caught up in the pussy. A bitch was quick to scream out they're pregnant just to get a grip on a baller's bag. Some even did it just to stake a claim on a mufucka. That was one of the main reasons Jamir kept a short leash on his dick. He was too young to let a bitch trap him with a baby, and he planned to keep it that way.

Danny put the condoms back in his pocket and then pulled out a small baggie of weed. He pulled the swisher sweet from behind his ear and smiled. Jamir watched as he split the cigar down the middle with his thumb nail and emptied out the contents on to the ground. He opened the baggie of weed and pinched a finger full and began filling the brown cigar paper back up. After he filled it with the potent Kush, he pulled out a baggie of crack and looked at Jamir.

"This shit sprinkled in your blunt is what's up. Have your dick hard as a mufucka. Make ya wanna knock the bottom out some good pussy."

"Nigga, what the hell is you talking about?"

Jamir looked on as Danny pulled out one of the rocks from the baggie and broke it up on top of the weed. He then rolled the cigar paper up and licked it to seal in its contents. Jamir wondered when Danny had starting geeking his blunts like that. He didn't want to pry because it wasn't affecting him, but he was bothered by the revelation.

The smell of the geeked up blunt made Jamir scrunch up his nose. He felt like he was about to throw up from the aroma. That wasn't his first time being around someone who laced their weed, but it never seemed to bother him like it was doing then. Maybe it was because of the disgust he felt as soon as he saw Danny's delightful attitude when he pulled out the crack. To Jamir, anyone who smoked that shit was a crackhead, and there was no other way to put it. It didn't matter the manner in which they chose to do it because it was all the same at the end of the day. When Danny tried to push the blunt his way, Jamir pushed it back in his direction. There was no way he would go out like that, after watching his own father do it for years. The thought alone pissed him off.

"Nigga, when you start filling your weed with that shit? The fuck is wrong with you?"

"Ah, it's not that serious. Tweaking a little bit of this shit ain't gonna do a damn thing. It ain't like I'm putting it on the pipe, so chill."

"You might as well put it on the pipe 'cause there ain't no damn difference between a pipe and a blunt. Your ass is still smoking crack. Next thing you know, you'll be somewhere down on your knees sucking a mufuckin' dick for that shit. What the hell are you thinking?"

"Fuck you, nigga. I ain't no damn crackhead, and I ain't gonna be sucking shit. The hell is all this coming from?"

Jamir reached over and pulled the half smoked blunt from between Danny's fingers and threw it down on the ground. He stood up from where he sat on the car's hood and stepped on it with his right Timberland, and then looked back at his boy.

"That shit right there will only lead to destruction. I know because my fuckin' pops did it and, just like you, it started off as nothing. Now his black ass is sitting in a prison cell and getting fucked by niggas that still have ties to the streets. He's they bitch, and he will do anything for that shit."

"Yeah, but I ain't your mufuckin' pops, Jamir. I know how to handle this shit. You ain't got nothing to worry about. Chill the hell out."

"Yeah? Well if you gonna continue to roll with me, you better handle it because I ain't about to let you or anybody else bring me down. I done came too far and worked too hard to get where I'm at for that to happen."

"A'ight, a'ight damn. I'll lay off it. You don't gotta worry about me doing it again. We cool on that?"

Jamir thought about it for a minute. He knew that Danny was lying because he was too comfortable with putting the crack in his weed, but he would try to give him the benefit of the doubt, as long as he never did it around him again.

"Yeah, D, we still cool. I just don't want to see you fall short of your glory. You better than that."

No sooner than he said it, a pearl-white Ford Explorer pulled up and parked beside Jamir's Buick. The ride was clean and fresh. It was something that Jamir could see himself pushing one day. However, no matter how much admiration he had for the ride, he wasn't familiar with it, so that meant he wasn't familiar with its occupants either. His hand automatically went to his waistline and made contact with the cold steel he kept there. He had put in a lot of work to get to the position he was in, and he wasn't about to let a mufucka pull a jack move on him. It wasn't until Danny stood and held his hand up that Jamir eased his hand off the weapon.

"Hold up, bruh. They ain't here for no jack move. They came down to show us some love."

"Nah, I'm good on love. I don't need a mufucka to show me anymore."

"Come on, Jamir, don't act like that. Just trust me on this."

Jamir wasn't sure what Danny was up to, but he decided to go ahead and see how shit played out. He would make sure to stay on alert. When two big, black mufuckas stepped out of the vehicle, Danny gave them both some dap. Jamir wondered how long he had been familiar with the niggas because he couldn't remember Danny ever mentioning them, or anyone else. Jamir saw the print of a gun sticking out from the biggest one's shirt and hoped it didn't become a problem because, in all honesty, he wasn't trying to catch a body. He still had so much to live for and was too young to be sitting in a courtroom fighting murder charges. He listened as Danny introduced the two men.

"This is Timbo and Bryan. They control the whole DMV circle and they been doing some big things up there. They trying to expand now, and they would like us to help them with that. They want to put us on and make this little ass city show up on the map."

The look on Jamir's face spoke volumes. He couldn't believe that Danny had gone behind his back and set something up like that. He could have at least had the decency to bring it up in a conversation, so they could have discussed it together. He knew that Danny was ignorant when it came to loyalty and respect, and he would make sure to check him about it, once they were alone.

"Nah, we already on, so ain't nothing y'all could do for us. Thanks for the offer, but we good."

Danny turned to Timbo and held up a finger, telling him to give him a minute. Timbo was the head of the DMV gang, and he was hard to get to. Danny had lucked up and didn't want the opportunity to pass him by. He pulled Jamir to the side to talk to him in hopes that he could change his mind. Danny didn't have the funds to invest on a new venture, so he needed someone to go in with him. He tricked off most of his money, and what he didn't use on tricking, he had to give to Trish to help take care of his son. He couldn't risk getting picked up behind some child support. He knew the county was hard on a nigga that didn't provide for his seed. Danny needed a come up, and these out of state niggas was willing to give him a chance. He couldn't allow Jamir to fuck it up.

"Yo, bruh, the fuck is your problem? We got a hell of an opportunity here, and you just gonna let that shit pass on by. We need this connection. Don't you wanna be bigger and soar to new heights? This is your chance to get on top. What's up with that?"

"Look at me when I tell you this and understand exactly what I'm saying to you. I don't work for nobody but myself. A mufucka won't ever get the chance to hold some shit over my head. I vowed that I would rise on my own, so that way, I wouldn't ever feel like I owed someone. Now if you wanna get down and join they team, so be it. But when shit don't turn out in your favor, don't come back to me crying."

"Damn, Jamir, it's like that, my nigga? I thought we was good, but now I see that this shit we been doing is one sided."

"Don't try to turn this around and make it seem like I ain't had your back because I done pulled you from a lot of shit. I don't need those mufuckas. But if you do, then ride the fuck on outta here."

"Oh, so I guess, since you done moved up a key, you on that big coke boy shit. My nigga, those pies you be whippin' up ain't gonna amount to shit when I get done. I guess I'ma have to show your ass how things are supposed to be. When I shut you down, don't come to me whining like a little pussy to put you back on. Peace out, my brotha."

Danny turned and walked away. Jamir watched him walk over to Timbo and Bryan and say something before he got in his ride and drove away with the two men following close behind. Jamir felt like nothing good was going to come of the situation, but he didn't have time to raise a man. He had other shit on his plate to deal with. As long as Danny didn't get in his way, he could let that flaw ass shit go. He shrugged that shit off and decided to go ahead and take it in for the night. Danny had made his own decision to switch out, and he could kiss Jamir's ass. There would be no second chances. Jamir shook his head in disappointment and opened his car door. Before he could get inside, a voice from behind him halted everything.

"Hey, Jamir, what's going on? You look a little down. Is everything okay?"

Jamir turned to face the voice. He knew whose voice it was because it was a melody to his ears. His heart sped up as soon as he looked at her. Rachel appeared to have just stepped out, which explained why he hadn't seen her all night. She was fresh in an orange and black Nike track suit. She even wore the shoes to match. He had to admit, she was a fly ass white girl. He hated to see her waste her potential on a crack pipe, and he hoped that one day she would find her true worth. Her concern for him meant a lot. He was happy that she'd showed up because he could definitely use a distraction from all the shit he had going on in his mind.

"I'm good, just got too many things going on in my thoughts. Nothing I can't handle, though."

"You in the mood for a little company? Maybe I could give you other things to think about and help ease the tension."

"Yeah, I guess a little company would be nice. Shit's been slow out here anyway. Come on and get in."

"You mean, you want me to get in the car right here, right now, while all these people are still out? Are you sure? I mean, I don't want to ruin your image or anything."

"Okay, I deserve that. Ain't nobody paying us any attention, so it's all good."

Rachel smiled and slid into the same seat she had been in before. She knew that he was uncomfortable being seen with her, so she wondered what had brought on the sudden change. She shrugged it off and decided not to question it because she was excited to just be in his presence again. The ride to his house was a very quiet one. The last thing Rachel wanted to do was disturb his peace, so she sat back and enjoyed the ride. When he finally pulled into his driveway, he looked over at her and stared. Her sweet scent lingered in the air and tickled his nose, and he couldn't wait to be inside of her again.

"Where you been all night?"

"Don't worry, Jamir. I haven't been with anyone else. I just didn't feel like hanging out, that's all."

"So what changed your mind?"

Rachel smiled. "You did."

Jamir didn't know what to do with what she said. Every female he had come across wanted something. If it wasn't money, it was drugs, or something else material. No one ever really wanted just him. He smirked and opened his car door. Hell, he had to do something to stop himself from laying her down right there and pushing some dick inside of her. She turned him on in the worst kind of way, and he couldn't control it. Jamir was already opening the front door and Rachel finally followed suit and got out of the ride. As soon as they got inside and stepped into the small bedroom, Jamir pulled out the dope he had in his pocket and sat it on the dresser. He would let her decide what to do with it.

"Here you go, ma. Take as much as you want. Do you."

"Nah, I think I'm good. I'm not really in the mood to get high tonight. I just want to chill out and spend some time with you, if that's okay."

"Yeah, that's cool. I mean, I ain't gonna watch you or nothing, if that's what you're worried about."

"No, Jamir, I'm serious. I want you to be my high tonight. Think you can do that?"

Jamir smiled and pulled her close. He stared deep in her eyes, without saying a word. He had a lot of shit on his heart and mind, shit that he didn't want to burden her with. He didn't want to give her false hope because, no matter how bad he wanted her, it just wouldn't work between them. He had to keep telling himself that so he could keep his feelings at bay. He wished that things could be different, but he knew nothing would ever change.

That shit Danny pulled on him had him in a fucked up mood. He wanted to tear something up, but he couldn't allow himself to take it out on her. She wouldn't understand, no matter how much she claimed to. Jamir slowly undressed her. He wanted to admire each and every part. He sat down on the bed as she stood in front of him. Her small pink nipples stared back at him. They were perfect and he couldn't help but pull one into his mouth.

"Oh, Jamir, that feels so good."

The way his name rolled off her tongue made his heart flutter with passion and made him suck a little harder. He reached between her thighs and inserted a finger in her wetness. Her hips rotated as he gently slid his digit in and out. When he pulled it out of her, he put it in his mouth and savored her creamy essence. He had never tasted anything so sweet. The taste of her was just a teaser and wasn't enough to satisfy his growing hunger, so he decided to put a bigger helping on his plate.

"Lay down, ma. A nigga got something special for you tonight."

When she laid down, he got undressed and climbed on the bed in front of her. She willingly opened her legs. Rachel was ready for the dick, but Jamir gave her something else. He kneeled between her legs and spread her neatly trimmed pussy lips. Her clit was hard, and he knew that once he sucked it into his mouth, there would be no turning back. He feasted on her sweetness until she couldn't take any more, and then, he filled her with the beast. He made love to her with so much passion and intensity that he even amazed himself. He was so confused at how she had the power to bring another side out of him.

When their lovemaking was over, Jamir pulled her into his arms and held her close. His connection to her was crazy. He had never felt so safe and so secure. It was a shame that it could only last for that moment. He didn't understand how something so wrong could feel so right to him. He hated it but knew he had to keep his feelings exactly where they were at, deep inside his soul.

"Damn, Rachel, a nigga really feeling you, but you know that we could never be out there like that. We got to keep this shit between us, no matter how good it feels or how deep it gets. You do understand why, don't you?"

"Ya know, Jamir, from the first time I saw you, I wanted you, but you never paid me any attention. There's just something about you that's different from everybody else. I don't even want to get high when I'm with you because you fulfill that desire. I'm not ashamed of anything I've done, and I need someone in my life that feels the same way. I don't want someone who is embarrassed by the things I've done. You don't want people to know but yet, somewhere inside of you, there's some feelings. So no, I don't understand."

"Come on, Rach. How the hell you expect me to feel? I don't know how many of them niggas out there you done been with. That shit would eat me up inside. Niggas you done fucked for that shit gonna be laughing in my face. I can't live like that. Shit would make me bitter as fuck. This shit we doing has got to stay on the low. You just gonna have to accept it as is or not at all."

Rachel sat up in the bed and turned to face him. She knew that she needed to get up and get the hell out of there, but her heart wouldn't let her. She didn't want to be just a piece of pussy to him, but if she wanted to be around him, that was what she would have to settle for. The words he had spoken hurt her feelings, but she kept it to herself. She had already exposed too much of herself to him and knew the more she gave, the deeper she would fall.

"Fine, Jamir. It's whatever you say. But since you only want me to be a trick, then you need to fuck me like one. Give me my shit, get your nut and send me on my way. You do understand why, don't you?"

The sarcastic comment was called for and one that he deserved. He knew he had hurt her, but he had to stand by what he said. He watched as she got up and put her clothes back on. Something deep inside of him wanted to stop her but he couldn't bring himself to do it. He knew it would be best to just let her leave, so he sat there and did just that. An emptiness filled the room once she was gone. He had never felt so alone until that moment. Jamir looked on the dresser and saw that she had taken the dope. She meant what she had said and there wasn't shit he could do about it.

Chapter 3

"So, what's the deal with ya boy? I thought you said he was gonna be down with the plan? Nigga, what the hell happened? I ain't make this mufuckin' trip for nothing. So start talking."

Danny couldn't lie, he was nervous as hell. He had assured Timbo that Jamir would be down to put in some work for them. He couldn't believe that he had turned the work down. Danny needed that plug because he had been spending money just as fast as he was making it. That come up was going to help him get back right, but thanks to Jamir, his plans had been fucked up. He had to convince him that it would be a good move for the both of them.

"Ain't shit happen but his mufuckin' ego. Jamir ain't used to working for anybody but himself. I've known him since we were kids, and he just needs a minute to think about it and absorb everything. Just let me sit down and talk to him alone. I got to make him see how we gonna benefit from all this. He'll come around."

"How can you be so sure that you can convince him because that nigga seemed like he wasn't down with a damn thing."

"Just chill, Timbo. That's my nigga, and if I don't know nothing else, I do know that he trusts me. He knows that I wouldn't step to him on no bullshit. Just give me a few days to talk to him and I'll get back up with you."

"A'ight, I'll give you that, but I got to get back up to the DMV by the end of the week, so don't be playing around. There's plenty of other niggas that would jump on an opportunity like this. Don't be the one it passes by."

"I got you Timbo. I give you my word."

"Yeah? Well you better hope I can count on it because I don't like my time to be wasted."

Timbo stood and nodded at Bryan, who stood by the door with his hand on his weapon, just in case he needed it. He had bodied many niggas for trying him and Timbo's gangsta, and he wasn't above bodying one more. Timbo knew his boy was ready to buss a cap, but he shook his head to let him know everything was cool. Not another word was said because all the cards had been put on the table. Until another play was made, the game was at a standstill.

Danny was relieved when Timbo and Bryan left the room he had rented solely for that purpose. There was no way he could have handled it at the apartment he lived in with Trish and their son. Too many questions would have been asked and he would be damned if he would have answered them. Trish's nagging ass stayed in his ear. If it wasn't for his seed, he would put that bitch to sleep.

Danny locked the room door and tried to figure out how he would convince Jamir that the move would be a good one. He thought that if he could see how much they could profit, he would be all in. Jamir had been on the come up for years, but his rise was moving slow. All Danny wanted to do was help him rise a little faster, but the mufucka thought he was too good to work under someone else. A real nigga knows they gotta crawl before they can walk but Jamir's ass acted like he came out of the pussy and stood on his own two feet. Danny wasn't sure what he would do if Jamir didn't take the bait because he didn't know of anyone else he could turn to.

He sat back on the bed and pulled the small baggie of rocks out of his pocket. He picked up the box of swisher sweets off the table and slid one out. He, once again, used his thumb nails to split the brown paper down the center and dumped the loose tobacco in the ashtray. The bag of weed was in the bedside table right next to the Bible, a book Danny had never read. He didn't have time to follow Jesus because he felt like the streets needed him more than he needed the Word.

Danny filled the empty brown paper with the weed, the same way he had done when he was on the block with Jamir. He thought about the disgusted look Jamir had given him when he broke off a piece of the crack rock and laced his weed with it. Who was that nigga to judge him? His ass wasn't perfect. Danny quickly became pissed off and instead of one rock, he pulled out two. He dropped the broken pieces on top of his weed and rolled the thick paper back up. He licked the paper to seal it and then put it between his lips. He lit the blunt and took a long pull. The smoke filled his lungs and took him to another place. At that time, a thought came to his mind. He smiled because he had the perfect idea. He knew there was one thing that could possibly make Jamir cave and as soon as he finished his blunt, he would take a ride and find it.

***

Danny turned on the block just in time to see Rachel walk up in old man Nate's store, so he pulled over to the side of the building and got out. He wasn't sure what she had gone in there for, but just in case it was to make some bread, he chose to stay outside. He didn't want to be the one to fuck up her hustle, so he leaned back against his ride and decided to wait it out.

Danny looked around and noticed KP and Smack at the small park that sat across the street. They were around the same age as him and Jamir, but for some reason, Danny felt like they had their shit together a little more than them. He would make it his business to knock them down a notch, once he rose to the top. A little further down the block was Blount and his partner in crime, Raw, a female gangsta who looked and acted more like a nigga than the niggas themselves. That bitch was smooth as a mufucka and had even finessed a couple of hoes right out from under Danny's grip. He couldn't be mad at her for wanting to feast on some pussy, he just wished she would have ate off of someone else's plate. Mufuckas still talked about how that bitch managed to pull that slick move and would often tease Danny and say that it was because Raw had a bigger dick than him. Danny truly felt like his player card had been fucked ever since. He would make it his business to pay that bitch back one day.

While Danny stood there scheming and thinking of ways to stack his paper, Rachel walked out of the store. He thought about how he saw her walk out of Jamir's back door. He never mentioned it because he felt like it was something he could possibly use against him one day. He had known for a while that Jamir had a thing for the white girl, but he could never get him to come clean. Danny didn't really give a fuck one way or the other. He didn't have time to be jocking another nigga's dick issues. Shit, to be honest, he had been wanting to stick his dick in the vanilla cream pie for a minute, but he had always ended up getting into something else. He decided that it might be a good time to seize the opportunity.

"What's up, Rachel? You feel like giving a nigga a little head or even some of that pussy? I got what you need right here."

Rachel looked at the baggie of rocks and shook her head. She couldn't believe how disrespectful Danny was to her. True enough, she had done sexual favors in exchange for drugs, but no one had ever made her feel so low. Danny had never tried her before, so she couldn't help but wonder if Jamir had put him up to it, just to see if she would fuck his right-hand. She couldn't lie, she did enjoy getting high sometimes, but it wasn't something she wanted to make a career of. People didn't know, but she often paid for her dope with money she got from writing bad checks. She didn't care whose checks they were because she had become a master forger and she'd rather risk going to jail for forgery than spreading her legs open for just anybody.

"No thanks, I'm busy right now. Besides, you know I'm not about to do anything with you because I don't fool with you like that."

"For real, bitch? You suddenly too good to suck a dick for a dime piece? Come on, Rach, if you worried about Jamir, I ain't gonna say shit to him. I'll keep it between us."

"What does Jamir have to do with anything? I don't answer to him or anyone else."

Danny stepped a little closer to her and bent down beside her short stature so he could whisper his next words. It wasn't that he really gave a damn about someone hearing him. It was all just for show. He hoped that it made Rachel change her mind.

"Look, I know you got a thing for my boy, but ain't shit gonna ever happen there. He just gonna keep sneaking you in the front door at night and out the back door in the morning. Mufucka only cares about his image. The last thing he wants is for these niggas around here to find out that he has some feelings for your crackhead ass, but a nigga like me is up on it. Jamir trying to keep that shit on the low, but not me. You suck this dick right and I'll give you anything you ever desired."

"See, that's why I would never fool with you. Everything about you is disrespectful."

Rachel turned around to walk away but Danny wasn't one to give up easily. He hoped his next words would sway her.

"A'ight then. You care so much about Jamir, how 'bout you help my boy rise a little higher? He ain't gonna tell nobody, but his black ass is struggling right now. I got the means to help him, but he don't want to listen to me. He thinks he can keep doing shit on his own, but the nigga could use some assistance. You convince him of that and I'll give you all the respect you asking for."

"What do you mean, help him rise higher? I think he is right where he wants to be. Jamir doesn't seem like the type of guy who even want to be out there like that. So no, I'm not gonna convince him to do anything. Even if I did, he's not going to listen to me."

"See, that's where you're wrong. I think you could have some influence on his decision. Just talk to him about it while he's deep in them walls. A nigga will agree to anything while his dick is leading the way."

"I can't do it, Danny. Whatever you're plotting, you're gonna have to do it alone. I don't want any parts of it. I don't know why you think I can do it, but me and him ain't like that. Get the thoughts of me and him out of your head because your feelings are wrong. I gotta go. Good luck."

Danny was so pissed, he wanted to punch the white bitch right in her mouth. But he couldn't afford to get cased up on no assault charges, especially on a white woman. He knew the judge would throw the book at him for that. He felt like Rachel was going to tell Jamir about their conversation, but he wasn't worried because he already had his lie put together. He finally got back in his ride and pulled out of Nate's with another destination in mind.

Danny was on his way to Jamir's house when his phone rang. He answered it, without checking to see who the caller was, but soon regretted his decision.

"Where the hell are you at, Danny? You were supposed to pick me and DJ up an hour ago. Don't let me find out you chasing behind some other hoe's pussy and that's why you ain't came yet nigga."

"Trish, shut the hell up. I was handling some business. Damn, I'm on my way."

"Yeah, well you better be or you gonna be laying that ass somewhere else tonight."

Trish hung up and left Danny on the line. He held the phone to his ear for a minute before throwing it in the passenger seat. He couldn't believe that he didn't check to see who it was before he answered. If he would have known it was Trish, he would have sent that shit to voicemail. He had grown real tired of her bullshit. Once he came up in the game, he would get his own place. If he knew that he could kill the bitch and get away with it, she would be somewhere stinking. He could find another one to help him raise DJ, one that wasn't so damn needy.

He pulled into the Big Little store so that he could turn around and saw Jamir's auntie, Mary. He knew there was no way that he could avoid her because she had threatened many times to tell Jamir that they had fucked. She even tried to put the baby she was carrying off as his, but he didn't believe that shit for a minute. He had worn two condoms when he ran up in her, just in case that pussy was burning. He still didn't want anyone else to know, and so far, no one did. He pulled up beside her and was shocked to see that her stomach had gone down. He wondered where the baby was.

"Damn, Mary, Jamir ain't say nothing about you dropping that load. Where the little mufucka at?"

"Now you know my nephew don't fool with me like that. Hell, he avoids me at all costs."

"Well maybe if you wasn't trying to suck his dick for that shit, he'd act different toward you. Have you ever thought of that?"

No, Danny, dicks were made to be sucked, no matter who they attached to. I was just trying to fulfill my duties as a woman, but Jamir acts like he too good for all that. I'm starting to wonder if the little nigga is gay because he ain't never got a girl with him."

"He is definitely not gay. Just because you don't see him with a female doesn't mean he ain't slangin' that dick to 'em. That's family, and you shouldn't be trying him like that. Shit, if you just want something in your mouth, I got what you need here in these boxers. You feel like getting in and breaking me off real quick? You know I'ma look out."

Mary got in his car and immediately reached over to unzip his jeans. She was always ready to do what needed to be done and didn't care where she did it at. Danny released the lever on his seat so he could lay back. Then he reached over to put his hand down Mary's shorts, but she stopped him before he could get too far.

"Uh-uh, Danny. It's still messy down there from having that baby last night. You gonna have to settle for playing with my nipples instead. I got you next time."

Danny pulled his hand back, and then slid it up her tank top. He released her breast and began twisting her nipple between his fingers. He noticed the white liquid squirt out and rubbed his fingers in it and then tasted it. He had never tasted breast milk before, but he could see why babies sucked the hell out of their momma's titties. Meanwhile, Mary sucked his dick and played with his ball sack. She was the only chick that could make him cum in less than two minutes. She was a pro at that shit and should teach a class on it.

"That's right, Mary. You sucking the hell outta that mufucka. A nigga 'bout to shoot off all in that throat. Get ready and open them tonsils up. Catch it, baby, catch it."

Danny gripped the back of Mary's wig and pushed her head down so he could release his unfertilized children. He didn't want to waste anything, especially on the seat of his car. As always, Mary didn't disappoint. She swallowed each and every drop. She even licked the edges around the head when she was done, just to make sure that she left nothing behind.

She wiped her mouth and held out her hand to get what Danny owed her. As soon as he zipped his pants back up, he reached in his pocket and handed her a rock out of the baggie. He would have given her two, but he had only three left until he could re-up. He wasn't about to cut himself short, so Mary would have to be satisfied with what he had given her.

"Thanks, Danny, you always look out for me. I give you my word, as soon as this pussy heals, it's all yours."

Mary opened the car door and got out. No sooner than she shut it, Danny's phone rang again. He checked the caller ID that time and saw that it was Trish again. But instead of answering, he sent her ass to voicemail. He didn't feel like dealing with her. If it wasn't for his son, he could have gone in another direction. Danny Junior meant everything to him, and he didn't want to be known as a deadbeat dad. He wanted to be someone his son could look up to and be proud, so he knew he had to be there for him as often as he could. With that thought in mind, Danny started his car so he could go across town and pick up Trish. He would check in with Jamir later that night, and hopefully, by then, the nigga would have a different attitude.

Chapter 4

Jamir sat alone in the back booth of the Hardees restaurant. He would have stayed at the counter with Missy, but he knew she would take forever to decide what she wanted. Then she would still end up getting the same thing she always did when they ate there. He told her what to order him, gave her a hundred-dollar bill and went to sit down. He enjoyed the time he was able to spend with his little sister, and since Hardees was her favorite place to eat, they always ended up there.

Missy was only sixteen, but if one didn't know, they would swear she was in her twenties. She had the body of a grown woman and the face of a super model. Her natural hair hung to the middle of her back. When she was a little girl, she swore that she would never cut her hair and, aside from the occasional trim, she had stuck to her word. It worried Jamir because he knew that grown ass men would walk past her and check her out with lust in their eyes. So far, she hadn't complained about one trying her, but it was bound to happen. Jamir could see himself killing a mufucka about her, but he always hoped that he wouldn't have to.

Jamir was lost in his own thoughts when Missy finally sat across from him. She waved a hand in front of his face and brought him back to reality.

"Uh, Jamir. Hello in there. It's your food talking. Where are you?"

"Sorry, sis, just got a lot of shit going on in my head right now."

"You wanna talk about it? My friends tell me all the time that I'm a really good listener."

"Now you know I don't involve you in my street shit like that. Besides, you too young to have to walk around with my burdens on your back. Focus on your shit and let me worry about mine."

"In case you forgot, Jamir, I'm about to be seventeen. I'm not a little girl anymore, so you don't need to spare me from your bullshit. I can handle it."

"Hey, watch your mouth. Words like that take away from your true beauty."

"Nigga, please. Can't nothing take away from all this. My man stays telling me how pretty I am. You know I love the compliments, especially when they're the truth."

"Hold up, what man are you talking about? You ain't tell me you had a man. When the fuck did that happen?"

"Well maybe if you were a little more involved in my life, you would be aware of what's going on in it. I mean, I know you out there doing your own thing, but you still have family that needs you."

Jamir didn't respond to her comment because he honestly didn't know what to say. He had been slacking when it came to her, but it was only to keep her out of harm's way. Niggas in the game enjoyed using family to pull a mufucka's strings, and Jamir would never be able to live with himself if something happened to her.

"Look, Missy, I'm just trying to do better for myself and for you. How Ma did us was fucked up, but we overcame that and moved on. I'm coming up in the streets and you got one year of high school left. You gonna be the first in the family to graduate and your big brother gonna make sure you got what you need to go to college and be somebody."

"College? Uh-uh, I ain't trying to do no more classrooms, once I graduate. I'm tired of going to school every day. I'ma sit back and let my nigga take care of me for a while. Shit, I need a break from the books."

Missy rolled her eyes and popped a French fry into her mouth. She couldn't believe that Jamir had the audacity to tell her what she was going to do with her future. It was her life, and she was going to live it the way she wanted, whether he liked it or not. She would allow him to think he had the upper hand so he would leave the subject alone, but in the end, she would get her way. She started to ask him if she could have some of his fries, but she noticed that his concentration went somewhere else. She turned her head to see what had his attention and was shocked at who she saw. She turned her head back to him, hoping to get the scoop.

"You sure looking at that white girl mighty hard, Jamir. You sweet on her or something?"

"Nah, just someone that be on the block. I talk to her from time to time."

"From the way you looking at her, seems like it's more than you're telling me."

"Aye, sis, I gotta get up outta here and handle some thangs. You cool to make it home, or do you need to be followed?"

"I think I'm sober enough to drive myself home. The fries didn't have that much of an effect on me. Besides, my big brother didn't buy me that cute little Nissan to sit in one place. I'll be fine."

Jamir reached in his pocket, pulled five bills off his stack of money and handed them to Missy. He knew he had her spoiled and tried to make sure she always had what she wanted. The thought of any other man taking care of her pissed him off, which reminded him that he needed to find out who she had been talking about. That nigga would have to see him about his little sister. He bent down and kissed her on the forehead, and then walked off. As soon as he hit the corner, he saw Rachel at the counter and walked over to her. She didn't know that he was behind her until he pulled a twenty dollar bill out and put it on the counter to pay for her food.

Rachel turned around, saw that it was Jamir and smiled a smile she tried to keep hidden. She was still mad at how he handled her the last time they were together, but there was no way she could play hard to get when it came to him.

"I can pay for my own food, Jamir. I don't need your handouts."

"Where the hell is all that coming from? Your ass still in your feelings about the other night?"

"No, you made things pretty clear about me, you, and feelings, so you won't have to worry about that anymore."

"Come on, Rachel, you need to understand the position I'm putting myself in. Just accept what I can give you and let that be that."

Rachel picked up her take-out bag without responding. She was too afraid that she would say the wrong thing. Things between them were challenging enough, as it was. Right before she walked out the door, she remembered the conversation she'd had with Danny. She didn't really want to be in the middle of whatever was going on between them, but she had to let Jamir know what his boy had tried to get her to do. No matter how many times Jamir hurt her feelings, there was no way she could be disloyal to him. She didn't know what other extremes Danny would go to in order to get what he wanted, so she had to look out for number one.

"Go home, Jamir, I'll be over there as soon as I'm done handling business. I got some things to tell you, and I can assure you, you are going to want to hear."

Rachel walked out before he could stop her. He watched as she got into another nigga's ride, and it made him want to smash something up. Jamir couldn't help but wonder if she sucked the nigga's dick with the same passion she sucked his. He imagined all the positions the mufucka had put her in, and it caused his hand to go to his weapon. True enough, Rachel didn't belong to him and could do what she wanted to do, but he didn't want her to belong to anyone else either. He would be sure to check her on that shit, as soon as he got her alone.

Jamir walked out of the restaurant and got in his Buick. Then he remembered that he didn't have anything to give her. His connect wouldn't be coming into town from Miami until later that night. And even then, he would still have to cook it up. Rachel had become unpredictable, so he didn't know if he should stop and pick her something up, or just give her some cash so she could get her own. He had always tried to make sure he never ran out, but the fiends had been coming at him left and right. He was well aware of the fact that he had the best shit on the block, and he made sure to keep his customers happy.

When Jamir pulled in his driveway, Rachel was sitting on his front porch, a bad move on her part. He got out of his ride and walked up the steps that led to his door. The cool evening breeze almost made him pause and fuck her right there where she sat, but he knew better than to push the limits that he had set forth. Rachel had already caused him to break so many rules, and he couldn't afford to break anymore.

Jamir opened the door without saying one word to her. He was still in his feelings about the nigga she was in the car with. He decided to take his anger out on the pussy and deal with the rest of the shit at another time.

"You know what to do, so go 'head and handle that."

Rachel knew exactly what he was talking about. Every time she was there, he made her bathe first. He just didn't know that it made her feel dirtier than what she really was. She had a good mind to turn around and walk out, but remembered that he hadn't invited her there. She invited herself. She could tell he was angry, and she knew why. But if he didn't want her to fuck other niggas, then he needed to handle his position and make her completely his. However, Rachel knew Jamir wasn't about to put his pride to the side for her, so she would continue to live her life the way she wanted to live it.

"Yeah, I know what to do, but I didn't come over here for all that. I only came to tell you about your boy, and to let you know I'm leaving town for a while."

"The fuck you mean you leaving town? How you gonna do some shit like that?"

Rachel didn't know if she should be flattered or not. Jamir seemed to care more about her leaving than what was going on with Danny. It almost made her want to change her mind about going anywhere, but she knew that she couldn't. She had to leave for her own good, and that was that.

"I'm going up to Virginia to stay with my sister for a while. I want to get cleaned up, Jamir. I'm tired of living like this. I mean, it's not like I have a reason to stay, unless you plan on giving me one."

Jamir knew exactly what she meant by the comment, but there was no way he could oblige her. His image meant too much to him, and his pride was so big it should have had its own zip code. He wasn't sure how he would handle her leaving, but he knew he couldn't give her a reason to stay.

"Aye, go 'head in the bathroom and handle ya business, and then we can talk. I need to know what you trying to say about my boy. Oh yeah, I'ma have to pay you in cash because I ain't had a chance to link up with my plug yet. You cool with that?"

"Fuck you, Jamir. I don't need you to give me anything. Matter of fact, go find another bitch to take care of your needs. I'm leaving."

Jamir didn't even try to stop her because, for some reason, he felt like she would turn around and come back, but he was wrong. He waited for hours, and she never showed back up. No matter how hard he tried, he couldn't fall asleep. Finally, around one o'clock in the morning, his cell phone rang. Aware of who it was, he answered on the first ring.

"Well it's about time, my nigga. A young gangsta sitting here hungry as a mufucka. I need you to tell me where I can get a good meal from."

Jamir sat up in the bed and listened as his connect told him where he was lodged at. Malcolm was in his mid-thirties and controlled several areas in the Miami drug trade. His father had passed him the crown, once he retired and moved to the islands. Malcolm had been born and bred to rule the empire, and so far, he had been very successful at it.

He met Jamir when he had to come to his town on a run one day. Most niggas were intimidated by his status and weren't bold enough to approach him, but Jamir wasn't afraid. He stepped to him with the money he had collected from the church. Malcolm could see the hunger in the young man's eyes and decided to give him what he asked for. The next time he came up from Miami, Jamir was waiting with even more cash than before. Malcolm was impressed and even tried to give him some extra coke on consignment. But he refused to take more than he could pay for right then. Jamir had always sworn that he would never let a nigga put him in debt. He'd rather just keep working his way up slowly than for a mufucka to be breathing down his back about owing them something.

Jamir pulled into the Holiday Inn and parked in the back, right next to Malcolm's E Class Mercedes. He got out and, although he tried to never covet what the next man had, he couldn't help but admire the cream-colored exterior. The electric sunroof lacked tint, like the rest of the glass on the ride, and the deep-dish twenty-twos shined like diamonds under the bright lights that surrounded the hotel.

Jamir walked to room two forty seven and looked around before he knocked. Malcolm would know it was him because they had a coded knock that only the two of them shared. Had one tap been off, Jamir would have been riddled with a barrage of bullets. Malcolm stayed cautious because he knew mufuckas envied his status. He understood though, because hate was all a part of the game.

Malcom was deep in the pussy when he heard the knock. He could feel himself about to nut and refused to let anything get in the way of that. Malcolm ran into the female on the way to his hotel. Something about the switch in her hips made his dick hard, so he pulled over and swooped her up. His wife, Iliana, never went on out-of-town drop-offs with him, just in case things didn't go as planned. He needed her to stay back, just in case a lawyer had to be called. Plus, it gave him a chance to dip in some out-of-town pussy from time to time. Iliana was of Cuban descent and was the most beautiful woman he had ever seen, but her sex game had become dry. Malcolm had grown bored with the same routine every time he needed a nut. Iliana acted like it was more of a chore than anything, so Malcolm found his pleasure elsewhere.

Malcolm knew from the sound of the knock that it was Jamir at the door, and he didn't want to keep the young up-and-comer waiting too long, so he gripped the ass cheeks of the female that was in front of him and fucked like his life depended on it. When he felt the head of his dick pulsate, he slammed into her one final time. He clinched the muscles in his ass tightly and held his position as he emptied his seeds into the condom. The pussy had been good and tight, and he would make sure to give the female a little something extra for her time. When Malcolm finally pulled out of her, he peeled the condom off of his manhood and handed it to her.

"Flush this for me real quick while I get the door."

Even though she felt like he had said it rudely, she reached for the used condom anyway, and walked into the bathroom to handle what he told her to do. She had to take a piss too, so she needed the break. She had been on her way to find a quick trick so she could smoke a little something when he pulled her over. The way he dressed and the car he drove screamed out of towner. Plus, he had major dope man written all over his face. She hadn't expected to stay as long as she had, but he made it well worth her time and energy. She decided to take a quick shower while he handled his business, and then give him one more nut. Hell, he deserved it because he made her forget all she was going through.

When Malcolm finally opened the door, Jamir had an attitude. He had come there to handle business and felt like he shouldn't have had to wait. He knew it was because Malcolm had a female under him. Every time he came to town, he'd pull one and fucked her till he left, but he usually took care of his dealings first. Jamir wondered why he did things differently that time.

"Damn, nigga, you couldn't pull out long enough to open the door? Had me standing out there looking crazy and shit. The fuck is up with that, playa?"

"Just chill, young homie, a nigga was at his peak and wasn't about to let you fuck it up. Your black ass ain't got shit else to do. Now come on in so we can get down to business because when you leave, I'ma knock the walls out that bitch."

"Damn, bruh, pussy that good? You usually want to handle what we got going on before you take a dip. You way off your game on this one."

"Yeah, I had to seize the opportunity. Had to pull her before someone else had a chance. And I'm glad I did because it was well worth it. Pussy and head game on point. Makes a mufucka like me wanna go ahead and pass her the whole sack."

The two of them shared a laugh and then got down to the matter at hand. Malcolm pulled out the drugs while Jamir unzipped the backpack that held the funds. Jamir's money had been stacking up like a Wells Fargo bank, and he had finally moved up to four kilos. He planned to go even bigger the next time. Malcolm's father had not only passed him the reigns to the organization, but also the connect, so he always had that pure Peruvian flake.

Jamir could see himself in Malcolm's shoes one day, or possibly in some bigger ones. He couldn't wait to run a kingdom and hold the key to the streets. The two men sat down at the small table so they could finalize their deal. No sooner than they did, Jamir heard the bathroom door open and went for his gun. He had been so focused on the bricks of cocaine that sat on the table that he forgot all about the female Malcolm still had there.

Jamir looked at the female and felt like his heart would explode right in his chest. He couldn't believe that it had been Rachel laid up under the nigga he was about to give his hard-earned money to. He wanted to pretend like seeing her didn't affect him, but Jamir had feelings that ran deep. The look in his eyes could commit murder. He wanted to blow a hole in the bitch's heart, but now he wondered if she really even had one.

"The fuck is you doing up in here?"

Rachel wanted to run back in the bathroom and hide. She just couldn't believe what was happening. Of all the people she could have turned a trick with, she had to get in the car with Jamir's people. She felt so humiliated, as she stood there with nothing but Malcolm's t-shirt on. She felt like Jamir would never fuck with her again, and he had every reason not to. She was suddenly glad that she was leaving town and wished she could get on that Greyhound at that very moment. The trip couldn't come soon enough.

Malcolm stood there confused as he looked from Rachel to his young protégé. He couldn't understand what was taking place, but he knew a mufucka needed to enlighten him.

"Young playa, you know this chick? You need to make me understand why you talking to my company like that. So start explaining."

"Nigga, I ain't gotta explain a fuckin' thing."

45

"Who the hell do you think you're talking to? You must have done lost your damn mind. Now tell me why the hell you tripping like this. She your woman or something?"

"Hell nah, this bitch could never be my woman. You can have her ass because she ain't nothing but a trick anyway. And from this night on, our business dealings are over. I'm outta here."

Jamir knew the words were like a slap in the face, but he didn't give a damn because she had gone there first with her actions. Rachel could kiss his ass. He wanted nothing else to do with her. He picked up his bag of money and walked out. There was no way he could have stood there and dealt with Malcolm because all he would have thought about was Rachel being up under him. Shit wasn't supposed to affect him the way it had, but his reaction told him that he needed to get his feelings in check. Jamir knew his decision to walk would be one that he regretted one day. Malcolm had been his plug from the beginning, and he never spent his money anywhere else. Rachel had put him in a bad position, and it fucked him up.

Jamir started his car and drove out of the parking lot with a lot of shit going through his head. He had sixty grand in a duffle bag on his floorboard and not an ounce of cocaine. As he steered his Buick down the streets of the west end, he tried coming up with a plan. He thought of all his options, and then remembered something. There was only one way he could think of to get back on his grind. It wasn't really a move he wanted to make, but he had no other choice. Jamir picked up his cell phone and dialed, and when the called party answered, Jamir got right to the point.

Chapter 5

Danny was about to pull a jack move when he heard his cell phone ring. He thought that it was Trish checking up on him, so he let it go to voicemail. He wasn't in the mood to listen to her bullshit, and he needed to have a clear mind when he ran up in the house he had staked out for hours. It didn't belong to a kingpin, but the nigga that lived there got paid. Marcel was a young, rich mufucka, who thought his shit didn't stink. Danny had tried to get down with his team on several different occasions, but Marcel told him that he was too weak. Now, all Danny wanted was to show that bastard what weak really was.

Danny sat quietly on the side of the street. The darkness of the night hid him in plain sight, and he paid close attention when Marcel walked out of the house. He turned around and kissed his bitch goodbye, and Danny rolled his eyes. Quiana was fine but she had a fucked up attitude. Bitch thought she was too good for the likes of him, and Danny planned on knocking her down a notch. He had tried to holla at her, but she had the audacity to laugh in his face, like it was a joke. He wondered what the fuck was so funny, so he had asked her.

"The fuck is you laughing at? What do you find so funny?"

"Your lame ass is what's funny. To think that I would actually give a low life like you a second of my time is hilarious. Nigga, you ain't even in my league. Marcel would chop you up and eat your ass for breakfast, if he found out you were even standing this close to me, so back the hell up."

Quiana laughed in his face a second time, along with her girls. The shit was embarrassing for Danny, but he tucked his tail and walked away. He swore he would give that bitch something she could really laugh at one day. He wasn't no ugly nigga by a long shot. His low-cut fade stayed fresh and edged on point, at all times. When he smiled, his pearly white teeth complimented his Lebron inspired beard that he kept neat and trimmed, and even though he didn't have a body like Adonis Creed, he was still chiseled the fuck up. His fuck game was his only downfall. That shit was whack and every bitch on the block knew it. He would only be in the pussy for three minutes and be done. The only ones that truly appreciated the dick was the tricks that he would pick up on a daily basis. They were glad that he was in and out of it with a quickness, so they could go on about their business.

Once Danny saw Marcel get into his tricked-out Chevy Impala and pull off, he prepared himself for his venture. He slid on the black cotton gloves. Because one could never be too careful, he slid on a pair of latex gloves over them. After his fingertips were securely covered, he reached under his seat and pulled out the cold steel he had gotten from an underground dealer. He thought about wearing a mask, but wanted Quiana to see who would be stealing her final breath. At first, he was going to let her live, but the more he thought about how she had dissed him, the angrier he became. The bitch didn't deserve to live another day.

Once he had everything he needed to pull off the jack, he opened the car door to get out. No sooner than his left foot hit the concrete, his cell phone rang again. He hated it when Trish blew up his phone like that. He had one of two options; turn the cell off, or answer it and curse Trish the fuck out. She was disturbing his groove, and he didn't like it one bit. He decided to go ahead and give her ass a piece of his mind.

"Yo, Trish, the fuck you keep calling me for? I got some shit going on right now, so cut the bullshit and don't call me again. I'll see you when I get home."

"Nigga, this ain't your bitch, so watch your fucking mouth when you're talking to me."

Danny recognized Jamir's voice and pulled his leg back up in the car. He closed his door so he could listen clearly to what he had to say. He wondered if Jamir had changed his mind about the deal he had propositioned him with. He hoped that's why he was calling. If it was, Danny wouldn't have to pull through with what he was about to do.

"My bad, bruh. I thought it was Trish nagging ass. You know she be sweating me and shit, when I'm out here in the streets. I didn't expect it to be you, but what's up?"

"I've been doing a lot of thinking and was wondering if your people from the DMV were still in town. I mean, I know I tripped on you and shit, but a nigga just gotta be careful these days. Neva know when a mufucka gonna snake you. You know what I'm saying?"

"I feel you, playa, and it's all good. But come on, Jamir. You my boy, and I ain't got nothing but love for you. I was only trying to look out, that's all. I'm the last person you gotta worry about snaking you."

"Yeah, I know, but I got so much shit going through my head. I just wished you would have mentioned the plan before ya peeps showed up. Anyway, why don't you swing by the crib when you through handling whatever it is you got going on? I'll holla at you about that business then."

"That's some real talk, my nigga. I was about to get at a bitch, but the pussy can wait until another time. You know it's always business before pleasure with me. See ya in a minute."

Danny disconnected the call with a devious grin on his face. He didn't know what had happened to make Jamir change his mind, but he was damn sure grateful. He figured he could save the jack move for a time when he really needed it. Thanks to Jamir's change of heart, Danny was about to level up, and it couldn't have come at a better time. He opened his phone line back up and dialed Timbo's number. He was anxious to tell him the news and was glad that he answered on the first ring.

"What up? I hope you calling me about something worthwhile, because if not, you wasting my mufuckin time."

"Sup, Timbo, a nigga like me ain't neva gonna waste your time. You ain't even got to worry about that. I just called to let you know that my boy got at me and he wants me to stop by and enlighten him on what we got going on. Told you he'd come around. And as soon as I find out the deal, I'll holla. Make sure you on standby."

"I stay on standby when it comes to that bread, so handle what you need to handle and get at me. Peace out, brotha."

Timbo hung up before Danny could say anything else, so he threw his phone in the passenger seat and started his engine. He was about to be a paid mufucka, thanks to Jamir. Once his pockets got on swole, he would begin breaking the haters down from they wigs to they socks. All those niggas that thought they were above him would be under him and live by his commandments. The streets wouldn't be ready because he was about to make them bleed cocaine and crack. He couldn't wait to get in the kitchen and cook up that work until his hands got numb. That's how real mufuckas in the game did the damn thing.

On the way to Jamir's, Danny passed by old man Nate's and saw Missy coming out of the store. He had always had a thing for her, but in the game he played, nigga's sisters were off limits. But he had never been one to play by the rules, and he wasn't about to start. He pulled in beside Missy's car and rolled his window down. Missy was about to get in the Nissan Maxima that Jamir had gifted her on her sixteenth birthday. When she saw Danny, she rolled her eyes. Not because she didn't like him, but because she knew they could never entertain anything between them.

Danny was fine as hell, but her brother would disown her if he found out she had an attraction to his boy. She had heard the rumors about his dick issues and wondered if they were really true. Missy was disappointed, thinking that she would never find out.

"What's up, Missy? You wearing the hell outta them jeans, making a nigga's stomach growl and shit. When you gonna let me fix a plate?"

"Danny, do you know that my brother will kill you if he found out you was trying me like that?"

"Yeah, but you and I both know that you ain't gonna say shit 'cause you like it when I come at you like that. I know you wanna ride this dick, so stop playing and hop in."

"Whatever, nigga. You give yourself way too much credit. I know you done heard the bitches talking about that three-minute dick you got. Sorry, but I don't have that kind of time to waste."

"Three minutes, huh? A bitch only saying that because they don't want no one else to get it. Besides, you ain't the type to listen to what the next bitch says, now are you? Why don't you get on in and find out for yourself."

"And what if my brother pulls through and catches me in your ride? How would I explain that?"

"Jamir at the house waiting on me, so I can assure you that he ain't gonna move without reaching out first. We got business to discuss, and you know how serious he gets about that shit. You can let me hit real quick and then I'll jet on over there, while you dwell on how good I felt inside of you."

Missy blushed and thought about what he'd said. Her pussy was already wet and the only thing that could take care of the problem was some dick. Her boyfriend, Tyson, was out of town and couldn't heal her ails, so she figured it couldn't hurt to use a substitute. If Jamir ever found out, she would deny it to the bitter end. Danny could tell by the look on her face that he was about to be inside of her. He didn't want to seem too excited, so he stayed calm until she spoke up.

"Alright, Danny, but you got to give me your word that Jamir won't ever find out. Even if he does, this dick better be worth it."

Missy went around his car and jumped in the passenger's seat. She looked over at him, smiled, and then averted her eyes down. She wanted to see what he was working with, so she boldly reached over and grabbed his dick, while he put the car in gear and drove off.

Danny wasn't about to put out no money on a motel room he would only be using for a short amount of time, so he drove to an abandoned house and pulled behind it. He had brought several chicks to that same spot, so he knew they were safe and wouldn't be disturbed. Missy looked at him like he had tried her. She couldn't believe he had taken her there. Missy was a bougie bitch and had grown accustomed to Jamir, and even Tyson, spoiling her. So to imagine being fucked behind a house that she knew crackheads frequented was a blow to her ego.

"What the hell you park back here for? Nigga, I don't give up the pussy behind crack houses. I am not that bitch. You can take me back where you got me from."

She crossed her arms and pouted like a little girl, but that shit didn't faze Danny. She was giving up the pussy or he was gonna take it. He ignored her comment and pulled the lever so his seat would lay back. Then he unzipped his jeans and pulled out the monster. Missy's eyes got big when she saw how endowed he really was. Suddenly, the thought of the house was gone from her mind. All she wanted at that time was for Danny to be inside of her, so she pulled her jeans down and mounted him. She didn't have to worry about panties because she had stopped wearing them when she met Tyson. Missy got on him reverse cowgirl and held on to the steering wheel as he slid in and out of her.

"Damn, nigga, this dick is good. Fuck me with it like you angry. I like that shit rough."

Danny grabbed the sides of her hips and went to work, but his job didn't last very long. It was only once he released his seeds inside of her that he remembered he didn't put on a condom. He couldn't afford for her to get pregnant and hoped that she was on birth control.

"Ah shit, you on the pill, right?"

"Well don't you think it's a little too late to ask me that? Shouldn't that have been your first question? Shit, Danny, why didn't you put on a condom? I ain't ready for no babies. I'm about to be seventeen and still need to finish school. I can't be raising no kids."

"Look, just stop at the store and pick you up one of them Plan B pills, a'ight? That should take care of it."

"Okay, well give me the money to buy it because they say them pills is expensive."

"Girl, I ain't got no money to be giving you. This is gonna have to be out your purse."

"Wow! Just when I was starting to think that you was a real nigga, you go and ruin it. You know what? Just take me back to my car so I can go handle that. I mean, the sooner the better, right?"

"Yeah, that's what's up. That pussy is what's up too. Shit tight and wet. Listen though, I don't want you to be giving it up to other niggas. That thang too good to be sharing with the boys. You hear me?"

"I hear you, Danny, but just so you know, you are only the second nigga I done been with. I ain't hoe-ish like that."

"And you better keep it that way."

Missy thought that Danny had some nerve by telling her what she couldn't do with her body. The pussy didn't belong to him. Jamir would never allow it. She had to admit that the dick was top quality, but the rumors she had heard ended up being true. Missy loved the feel of a man inside of her, but she needed one that could hang. When Danny pulled up beside her ride, she opened the door to get out, but not before she left him with some parting words.

"Ya know, Danny, I hate to be the bearer of bad news and tell you that the rumors are true. You should really work on that before you step to me again. I don't like to be disappointed."

The words she said didn't affect Danny at all. He had gotten what he wanted and that was all that mattered to him. He hoped that Jamir never found out because that would definitely draw a bridge between them. No sooner than thoughts of Jamir came to his mind, his cell rang again. Instead of answering, he drove away from old man Nate's and headed to the bottom of the hill, so he could find out if Jamir was in or not.

Chapter 6

While Jamir sat and waited for Danny to come through, thoughts of Rachel invaded his mind. He was still trying to process and get over the scene he had witnessed. Of all the mufuckas she could have found to turn a trick with, she had to end up with the connect. True enough, she didn't belong to Jamir. But when she walked out of that bathroom with that nigga's t-shirt on, it had fucked his mental completely up. It would have been difficult for him to deal with Malcolm after that, even if the nigga didn't know any better. Even if he did, Jamir couldn't help but wonder if it would have made a difference. He decided that the best thing for him to do was cut ties and find someone else to deal with.

As much as Jamir was against it, he ended up calling Danny anyway. Hell, he didn't have time to sit around and wait for another mufucka to put him on. His money had been hard earned and, in order to see better results, he knew he had to put it back out there. Jamir wasn't familiar with the niggas Danny had tried to push his way and hoped that he didn't get into any bullshit behind it. He would take his chances just one time and see what the outcome would be. If things didn't add up right, somebody would be swallowing a hollow tip.

Jamir was in the mood to cause some damage and the only thing he knew he could assault, without catching a battery charge, was some pussy. As soon as he handled the business with Danny, he would go and scoop up Erica, a bitch who had been on his jock for a minute. She wasn't really his type, but the niggas on the block said she gave up the goods easy, and that was good enough for him. Erica was a thick ass redbone, but the bitch didn't have any class. Jamir liked his women smart. He said that a fat ass and big breasts could be bought, but common sense and book knowledge was hard earned. He rubbed his dick at the thought of catching a good nut. But in the back of his mind, he knew fucking Erica wouldn't satisfy a damn thing.

The sudden knock at the door brought him back from fantasy land. Jamir stood up from the couch and unlatched the front door, so he could let Danny in. When he saw him, he wondered why the nigga was in all black. Jamir was about to question him, but thought that it would be better not to know.

"Damn, nigga, the fuck took you so long? I been waiting on your black ass for over an hour. You acting like handling this business ain't what you wanna do. What's up with that?"

"Aw, Jamir, you know how them bitches be when they feigning for the dick and won't take no for an answer. She made it hard for a nigga to put that shit on hold. This dick too damn good to her. Bitch pushed me down on the bed and rode me like I was a bull at the rodeo."

"You crazy as hell, D, because unlike that bullshit, we all know you can't hang in the ring. That being said, you should have been here a while ago."

"Fuck you, Jamir. You don't have a clue as to how long my dick can hang, so go 'head on with that shit. Besides, your bitch ain't complain."

"Yeah, but that ain't my bitch no more. You can have her ass, nigga."

The conversation reminded Jamir of Brandy, a bitch he almost caught himself catching feelings for. At first, she seemed modest and respectful. Jamir thought she could have actually been wifey, but then he began to hear little things about her. Niggas around the way had a lot to speak on when it came to her. Jamir liked her so much, he almost looked past all that was being said, until he showed up at her crib one day. He walked to the back of her mom's house like he always did, so he could crawl through her bedroom window. But when he opened the curtains and peeked his head through, he saw something he didn't expect. Danny was laid back on the bed, while Brandy rode his manhood. The bitch looked like she was lost in pleasure and never even heard Jamir climb all the way through the window. She didn't know he was there until he hauled off and punched her in the back of the head. He hit her so hard, she fell off the dick and on to the floor. When she looked up and realized she had been busted, she began to cry. Little did she know, her tears meant nothing to Jamir. He just shook his head and turned around to go back out the same window he had crawled through. He and Danny never spoke of that night, but Jamir made sure to never underestimate a bitch again.

"Shiiiit, that hoe belong to everybody now. At least you found out she wasn't shit early in the game because, nigga, your soft ass was feeling that bitch."

"Yeah, I was feeling her, while she was feeling every mufucka with a dick. Stank ass hoe can't never come my way again. But yo, I ain't call you over here to talk about a bitch. I'm trying to do some business. I know I tripped on you and your people earlier, but that was my bad. Looks like I'ma need that connection after all."

"Oh, so you done came to your senses. But what happened to your people?"

"Ain't nothing worth discussing. Things just stopped working out, that's all."

"A'ight, if you say so. I'll give Timbo a call and let him know that you changed your mind. I'm telling you, bruh, you making a smart move."

"Yeah? Well, this shit you putting me on better be legit because I'd hate to have to rock ya peeps to sleep. Simple minded ass niggas will get got. Know what I'm saying?"

"Yeah, yeah, yeah, I got you, Jamir. But you know I ain't about to bring in a nigga that's gonna cause tension in the camp. That ain't what I'm about. Shit, me and you been down a long time. I ain't about to switch up on you now."

"Well, you do what you need to do. Give me a call when that nigga's ready, but make sure you let both they asses know that I don't work for nobody. I bring them the money, they bring me the product. No strings attached. I ain't obligated to do shit else that I don't choose to do. You feel me?"

"I feel you, Jamir. I'll make the call and set everything up."

"Well, I need that set up as soon as possible. So make sure your people understand I don't like to be put on hold. If that happens, I can find somewhere else to shop."

"I'm on it. Just chill and wait on my word."

Danny turned around and walked back out of the house to go on his mission. He knew that he had to make it count, and he would, by any means necessary. Meanwhile, Jamir picked up his keys and got in his ride. He knew exactly where to find Erica. He drove to a popular corner hangout called The Y. there was always something going on at The Y, but Jamir didn't like to hang out there because of the crowd. When he pulled up, all eyes turned to him. Jamir wasn't sure that he even wanted to get out, so instead, he rolled his window down and talked to the nigga that was closest to him.

"Aye, playa, that hoe Erica around here?"

The nigga took a sip of his Old English 800 and turned to Jamir. "Yeah, that trick inside. You wanna holla at her?"

"Bet that up. Can you get her for me?"

"You want me to walk up in there to fetch you a hoe? The fuck is wrong with your legs, nigga? Do you see me carrying a mufuckin leash?"

Jamir thought about what the man had said and laughed. He wasn't comfortable getting out of his ride and walking inside, so he did the only thing he thought would work.

Money made even the toughest of niggas move, so Jamir reached in his pocket and pulled out a knot of bills. He then peeled off a fifty and held it out to the man he asked to go inside for him. At first, the nigga looked at him funny, but ultimately grabbed the fifty and pocketed it before Jamir had a change of mind. Once dude walked off and went in, Jamir became paranoid of his surroundings. He felt like minutes had passed when it had really only been seconds. Feeling like the dude had got him for his cash, he started his car back up. Right when he put it in gear, Erica walked out.

She was dressed in some cut-off jean shorts that left the bottom of her ass cheeks exposed. Jamir could tell through the sheer tank top that she didn't have on a bra. He had always thought that it was a disrespectful act for a female to walk around exposed, but she wasn't his bitch, so he let it slide. The cheap looking sandals on her feet showed off her painted toenails. Jamir liked a woman with pretty feet, but even with polish, Erica's toes looked beat down. He had thought about pulling off, but she had his passenger door open before he could even put his foot on the gas.

"Hey, Jamir. Clifford said you were out here looking for me. It's about time you came to your senses and hooked up with a real bitch. I knew one day you'd come around."

"Yeah, well, I'm just trying to chill for a couple of hours, that's all."

"You mean, you ain't ready to make me your woman?"

"Hell nah, I ain't trying to claim nobody. Besides, when I settle down, it's gonna be with a lady. With you dressing like that, you're far off from being one."

"Well, Jamir, for a nigga like you, I'll change everything. Besides, when you become the king of the streets, you're gonna need a queen like me by your side. I'm that bitch that will hold you down and cool you off when things get hot."

"You talk a good game, but let's see what else that mouth can do."

Erica smiled and slid closer to Jamir. She unzipped his khakis and reached her hand inside. She raised her eyebrows and pulled his manhood out. Erica had always imagined how big it was, but she never really thought it would be that grand. No sooner than she put it to her lips, she felt the car come to a stop. Jamir put the car in park and killed the engine. Erica started to lift up to see where they were, but he pushed her head back down, so she could finish what she started.

"Don't worry about anything outside of this car right now. Just go 'head and finish off what your hot ass done started."

Erica did what he said and went back to work. He leaned his head back and listened to the sounds she made while she swallowed his length. It turned him on even more. He had to admit, the bitch could suck the hell out of a dick. He wondered what else she could do that good. So as soon as he emptied his nutsack down her throat, he pushed her off of him.

"Aye, go 'head and step out. I need you to go get us a room."

Erica looked around and saw that they were parked at the Budget Inn. She couldn't believe that he had taken her to the cheapest motel in town. She felt like she deserved better than that. She scrunched up her face and looked at Jamir like he had lost his mind.

"Uh-uh, Jamir. I'm not going up in that cheap ass, roach infested motel. This the place niggas bring tricks to just get a quick nut. Why you can't take me to your house? You really trying me right now. Besides, you ain't gave me no money to pay for a room. I know you not expecting me to pay for it."

Jamir shook his head and went in his pocket. He pulled out his knot of bills and peeled off a fifty. "Here. Take this and go get the room, and you can go ahead and keep the change for your troubles."

Erica looked at the fifty like it was foreign and sucked her teeth. She put the money in her bra and stepped out of the vehicle. She had thought about leaving Jamir in the car and walking back to where he got her from, but because she had wanted him to fuck her for the longest, she decided to do what he had told her. Once she got the room key and put the remaining eighteen dollars back in her bra, she walked back to Jamir's car. As soon as he saw her, he stepped out of the vehicle. He was about to ask her what room number, but she had a few choice words of her own that stopped him.

"You know what, Jamir? You got a lot of nerve to bring me here and talk about keep the change. Nigga, there is only eighteen dollars left. The hell do you expect me to do with that?"

"Come on, ma, stop trippin' on a nigga. You know you been feigning for this dick, so what you showing out for?"

Erica blushed because she knew that Jamir was right. Plus, he was just so damn fine. She had wanted to give him the pussy for so long and couldn't wait to get him inside the room. She would make damn sure that he enjoyed every minute with her because she didn't want it to be a one-time thing. She needed to make sure he kept coming back for more. Hopefully, it would be so good to him that he would make it official between them.

Erica led the way to room 142 and opened the door. The smell of stale cigarettes and crack made her want to vomit, but she managed to hold it in. The last thing she wanted to do was turn Jamir off, so no matter how much the stench upset her stomach, she played normal.

Jamir walked into the room behind her and locked it. He watched as she sat on the bed and posed like he was there to take her picture. But Erica had the game fucked up. He wasn't there to waste time. He was there to fuck and move on. He kicked off his Nike's and then stripped out of his clothes. His dick was semi-hard as he walked the short distance to the bed, where Erica sat, still dressed.

"The hell you still dressed for? Come on out that shit and get to work on this dick."

"Damn, Jamir, you just get straight to the point. I was hoping we could just chill and talk for a minute before we start."

"What the fuck you mean talk? We ain't got a damn thing to talk about but this nut. I mean, if you don't want to hang just say so. I'm sure that I can go find another bitch who wants to be where you at."

Erica scoffed but got up off the bed and stripped off what little bit of clothes she had on. As soon as she was naked, Jamir reached his hand between her legs and pushed a finger inside her wetness. He stroked it twice and pulled his finger back out and placed it under his nose. He winced at the odor and looked up at her.

"Yo, ma, you need to go on in the bathroom and wash that shit."

"Nigga, please, this pussy is clean, so miss me with that shit."

"Aye, for real, you a little musky down there, and I ain't about to stick my dick in no musky ass pussy. Just go soap up the rag and take care of that smell real quick. Come on, Erica, daddy gonna be waiting on you."

The comment made her smile, but deep inside, she still felt some kind of way about him saying that she had an odor. No one had ever made that kind of comment to her before, and she felt embarrassed. She knew that she should have showered after she had got done fucking Clifford, but she chose to hang out instead. She never could have guessed that Jamir Marshall would come looking for her. She told herself that from that day on, she would be on point.

When Erica was finished cleaning herself off, she walked out of the bathroom and back in the room where Jamir was laid back on the bed, a pillow propped up behind his head. He motioned for her to come to him, and she didn't hesitate. Erica couldn't believe that her biggest wish was about to come true. The anticipation had her dripping wet and ready to take all he had to offer. She crawled up on the bed beside him and spread her legs open.

Jamir got on his knees in front of her, his dick standing at attention. She reached down and began to play with herself but stopped as soon as she saw him tear open the condom package.

"Damn, Jamir, why you gotta ruin the mood? I'm trying to feel the real deal, not some stank ass latex."

"Don't worry, I could put on five condoms and you'd still feel it. This is as real as it gets with me. So take it or leave it."

"Whatever, nigga. Just do you."

Jamir shook his head, pulled on the condom, and then he put her legs on his shoulders. The buck had always been his favorite position because he could get deep. Once he had a leg on each shoulder, he pushed his hardness into her with one quick thrust. He felt her flinch underneath him and that he had hit the bottom of her womanhood. As he began to stroke, thoughts of Rachel came to his mind. He was still pissed at her and planned to take his anger out on Erica's pussy. His mind went to black as he punished her walls. The sweat dripped from his forehead on to her bare breasts as she moaned and begged for more.

"That's right, Jamir, this your pussy. Give me more, baby. Fuck me harder. Shit. Yeah. Yeah, Jamir. Fuck me."

The sound of her voice brought him back to reality, and he opened his eyes and looked at her. A disgusted feeling came over him, but instead of stopping, he pushed on until he finally released his seeds into the latex. Once he was finished, he pulled out of her and got off the bed. Erica watched as he walked into the bathroom and shut the door. A minute later, she heard the toilet flush and then the shower turned on. She decided to get up and go get in the shower with him, but she found the bathroom door locked. She realized that Jamir was a rude ass mufucka, but in order to be in his life, she knew that she would have to take him as is. She would be patient because she felt like he would eventually come around.

She stood at the bathroom door until the shower turned off, and then she ran back to the bed. Jamir walked out of the bathroom with a towel in his hand. He dried off, without saying one word to her. It was only when he picked up his clothes off the chair that he spoke.

"Aye, you staying here for the night, or you got somewhere you need me to take you?"

"You mean, that's it? You just gonna get your nut and leave me?"

"Hell yeah. You knew what it was when you got in my ride. Now you staying or leaving? I ain't got all night."

"So what if I decide to stay? You gonna come back and spend some more time with me? Ya know I still got some energy in me, just waiting to come out."

"Well you gonna have to use that energy on somebody else because I got shit I need to do."

Jamir tied his shoelaces and reached back in his pocket. He pulled out his knot once again and peeled off a hundred-dollar bill. He would have handed it to her, but he felt like she was too comfortable with him. He wasn't trying to make her at ease because, honestly, she didn't mean shit to him. He had only needed to release some pent-up pressure, and that was it.Jamir laid the money on the table beside the ashtray and put the rest back in his pocket. He turned and looked at Erica one last time and then walked out of the room. Without a second thought, he got in his ride and drove away from the motel, not once taking the time to look back. He decided to go home and wait to hear from Danny because he needed to get his grind on. And this time, he would grind harder than ever before.

Chapter 7

Bryan was leaned back against the side of the black, tricked out Cadillac STS, while Timbo sat in the back seat, nursing a kush filled blunt. Danny was amazed at how much Bryan kissed Timbo's ass and wondered if the two of them had something more going on. He had met plenty of niggas that were hard core, tatted up thugs with plenty of fat ass hoes on they side, but in all actuality, they wanted the same thing the hoes wanted, dick. He laughed at the thought and was curious as to which one was the bottom. Danny couldn't stand punk ass mufuckas. He thought they were disgusting, but it seemed as if that shit was everywhere. It was as if it was the new normal, but it was something he could never get down with. He thought that it was to each his own and it only left him with more pussy options.

Danny got out of his ride and walked up to Bryan. The nigga had never been one to speak much, so he stood like a statue. His dark soulless eyes gave Danny chills, so he looked away. All one had to do was mention Bryan's name and niggas would become spooked. His name had held weight in the game for many years, even before he hooked up with Timbo.

"Sup, Bryan? Why your big ass standing there like a statue? Looking like mufuckin Cujo and shit. Open the door, nigga. You know what it is."

Bryan didn't even respond to Danny's comment. Instead, he turned around and opened the back door for him. Danny hesitated at first, but then finally got in the back seat, where Timbo waited on him. Once he was inside, Bryan slammed the door shut, and then turned and stood in the same position he had been in before. Timbo didn't waste one second. He was a businessman and was quick to have a mufucka killed for wasting his time.

"You called and said you needed to see me, so get to talking."

"I told you that I was gonna reach back out to my boy and I did. I'm always a man of my word, and I came here with some news you gonna like."

"So stop all that small talk and tell me what's up."

"Well, it turns out that something happened between my boy and his connect. Now he needs a new one. I tried to get him to tell me what was up, but the nigga ain't wanna share no info. Anyway, he told me to contact you and see what the deal was, but he wants it to be straight from money to product. No strings attached."

"So what exactly is ya boy looking to spend? I need to know that it's even worth my time, especially if he don't plan on hanging. I need workers that can move my shit around the globe, and I usually only give to those who can contract they life to me, just in case something goes wrong. I'm all about the next man eating, but I ain't gonna put no more on their plate than mine. Know what I'm saying?"

"I know exactly what you saying, but Jamir ain't gonna bend on that. He would rather pay full price and keep all the profit than to get a discount and share the cut. He ain't about to call the next man 'boss', that's just how he is."

Timbo got quiet and thought about what Danny had said. He needed hungry niggas like Jamir. They were the ones that benefited him the most. He felt like young up and comers weren't as smart as the veterans in the game. Their only goal was to keep a flow of bills in their pockets to impress the bitches in the clubs. They didn't think about investments for the future because they only lived in the here and now. But

Timbo sensed something different in Jamir as soon as he met him. The young nigga was smart and would be a hard one to pull anything over on. Jamir was a go-getter, and even though Timbo respected that, he knew that it would also make him the competition one day. He needed Jamir to trust him. In order for that to happen, he would have to abide by his terms until he could make him change them.

Timbo needed the deal more than anyone knew. He had acquired a debt to the Colombians and was having trouble delivering. The money that Jamir could bring him would help put a dent in that debt. Jamir had status and the respect of the streets. Timbo could already see his rise in the game because Jamir was destined to be the boss one day. Whose boss was undetermined, but it would definitely happen. He'd be damned if he let the young thug surpass him when he had been at it for years.

Timbo was a show and tell nigga. He liked the fancy cars and the name brand clothes. He also liked foreign women, but they were expensive to care for, so he had to find those that were down on their luck. He had got his hands on Nadia through a sex trafficker. She had only been seventeen at the time, but he didn't care about her age. He planned to groom the Russian beauty into a queen that was fit for a king like him. Six years later, she was more beautiful than ever. He wanted to keep her that way, but in order for that to happen, he had to keep his status.

He had been trying to get her pregnant for a few years, but it just didn't happen. Timbo was pushing forty and needed a son to carry on his name. He wanted to plant as many seeds as he could, while he was still in his prime, but little did he know, Nadia didn't feel the same. She made sure to stay up on her birth control methods because she wasn't trying to be locked down with a baby on her hip. She would pretend to be disappointed whenever the pregnancy tests would come back negative, but deep inside, she was ecstatic. Thankfully, Timbo never caught on.

Nadia had become accustomed to being spoiled and getting whatever she wanted, no matter the expense. The last thing she needed was a crumb snatcher to share the wealth with. She knew that if Timbo ever found out that she was the reason they hadn't had a baby yet, he would make her pay dearly, so she was very careful not to ever get caught taking a pill. If Timbo wanted a son, he would have to find another bitch to have him. And deep down in her heart, Nadia wished he would.

"A'ight, I'ma deal with your boy, but I want thirty a key."

"Thirty? Nigga, you got to be crazy. Jamir would never go for that shit. You trying to tax the hell outta his ass."

"It's thirty or it's nothing. He can decide which one it's going to be. Now get out of my shit. I got things to do."

Danny shook his head and opened the door to get out. He turned and looked at Timbo as if he had something else to say, but he was really hoping that he would tell him that he was just bullshitting. When Timbo sparked up the blunt he had been smoking on, Danny knew that what he'd said was final, so he got out of the car and slammed the door behind him. Bryan gave him an angry look and then placed his hand on the butt of his gun. Danny held his arms up in surrender because he knew Bryan would pop off in a second.

"It's good, mane, it's all good."

Bryan didn't remove his hand from the weapon until Danny got back in his own ride and pulled off. Then he too got in the front seat of the STS. He looked in the rearview mirror at Timbo, who only nodded his head at him. Bryan knew what the head nod meant, so he pulled off and headed to the DMV, where they would package up what was needed for the deal Timbo had just made.

***

Danny drove to Jamir's house but regretted it as soon as he pulled up and saw Missy's car on the side of the street. He

68

didn't like to be around his boy when she was around because he was afraid that one day, the fact that he'd been fucking her would show on her face. He knew females liked to talk, but if Missy wanted him to keep sticking dick to her, she had better keep quiet. The last thing he needed was for something to mess up the deal he had made for Jamir. If that happened, he would have nowhere else to turn.

As soon as he got out of the car and walked up on Jamir's porch, the front door opened. Missy stood there with a smile on her face, but Danny tried to play it cool, as if her presence didn't bother him, but it was really fucking with his head. He looked her up and down, and then licked his lips because no matter how hard he tried, he just couldn't help himself.

"Sup, Missy? Where ya brother at?"

"He sitting in the kitchen eating. You hungry? I cooked up a little something. You more than welcome to get a plate."

Danny nodded his head and whispered in her ear, "A nigga like me stay hungry, but what I wanna eat ain't up in that kitchen. Why don't you holla at me later so you can feed me."

"I think I can do that. I got something real tasty for you to enjoy."

"Bet that up, ma."

Missy smiled, shut the front door, and then followed Danny into the kitchen, where Jamir sat at the small, round table, eating a plate of food. She knew that he wouldn't talk business in front of her, so she would use it as her excuse to leave. She would text Danny and tell him her location so when he was done, they could meet up.

"Don't mind me, fellas, I'm about to leave. I got a little shopping to go do."

Missy kissed Jamir on the cheek and held her hand out. It didn't matter that she already had money of her own, she wanted more, and she knew that he wouldn't turn her down. She smiled when he leaned back and reached into his pocket. Jamir pulled out the small wad of bills and peeled off three hundred dollars and passed it to her. Missy looked at him like he was crazy and then crossed her arms over her chest with attitude.

"Come on, Jamir, really? What am I supposed to buy with that? You know that I can't walk around in anything without a name on it, and that is not enough to buy a name."

Jamir shrugged his shoulders and put the bills back in his pocket. He didn't care that it pissed his little sister off. He needed his money to use for a re-up. Because he didn't know what Timbo was gonna ask for, he had to be really careful about what he spent. He had the feeling that the nigga was gonna tax him, but he didn't want to seem pressed up about it. He picked up his fork so he could finish his food, and wondered when Missy had become so ungrateful. After all they had endured growing up, he thought she would be a little more appreciative about how far they had come. He'd be sure to call her on it the next time she came over.

"Here ya go, ma. I got a little something to go with that."

Danny reached in his pocket and pulled out a fat wad of bills. He peeled off five one-hundred-dollar bills, handed them to Missy, and put the rest back in his pocket. Only he knew that the wad of money was a bunch of ones rolled up under the hundreds to make it look like he was balling. Giving Missy those bills put a big dent in his savings, but he wasn't worried about it because once the deal was made with Jamir, he'd be stacked up. Danny's plan was to tell Jamir that Timbo wanted thirty-two a key so he could keep that extra two grand for himself. He wasn't about to be left behind in the game, so if he had to skim off his boy's stash, then so be it.

Danny knew he had fucked up as soon as he saw the confused look on Jamir's face. He knew that as soon as Missy left, questions would be asked, and he could only hope that he had the right answers. He watched as Jamir pulled the three hundred-dollar bills back out. Once he handed them to

Missy, she thanked both of them and walked out. As soon as the front door slammed closed, Jamir's interrogation began.

"The fuck is up with you and Missy?"

"What the hell you talking about Mir? Ain't shit up with me and her. Dawg, you trippin' on a nigga and shit."

"Nah, I ain't tripping. I'm trying to figure out when you started giving up the bread so a bitch can go on a shopping spree. Niggas only do that shit for a bitch they fucking with, so what's up? Something going on with you and my sister?"

"Bruh, you my boy and I would never disrespect you like that. Missy like my little sister, too. We may not be blood, but y'all my only family. I would never try her or you like that."

"Yeah, well don't ever let me find out anything different. You my folk, but I will murk your ass about my sister."

There was a moment of silence between the two and a sudden awkwardness. Danny knew that Jamir would fuck him up if he ever found out about him and Missy. As bad as he wanted to call it quits with her, he knew he couldn't. Missy would sing like a bird if he left her alone. Then he would have a war on his hands, one he already knew he wouldn't win. As Jamir sat and stared at him with an unsure look on face, Danny decided to move past the conversation about Missy. He had gone there for business purposes, and he decided that it was time to get down to it.

"Aye, bruh, let's put all that bullshit aside and talk about some real happenings, like the deal I made for you with Timbo."

"A'ight, so what's up with that? What type of bread that nigga talking about?"

"He wants thirty-two a key. I tried to sway him lower, but that mufucka wouldn't budge. He pressed up because you won't work under him."

"The fuck I look like working under another man? I been working to get where I'm at since I was a jit, and I ain't about to let a bitch take that from me. I'm my own boss and call my own shots. A nigga like me ain't about to walk around and answer to someone, like they my fucking daddy. Fuck that mufucka. Tell him he can either lower that deal or he can kiss my black ass."

Danny knew that Jamir wouldn't like the sound of the deal he had made, but he didn't expect him to be so angry that he would call the deal off. He thought Jamir would be desperate enough to take whatever was put on the table, but he had clearly thought wrong. Danny tried to figure out what to do next, so he pushed his greed to the side and told Jamir the real numbers.

"Aye 'Mir, I know that shit sound crazy and that's what I told him. I don't know mane, I could try to get him to at least thirty, but that might be the best I can do."

"Nah, let me holla at that bitch ass nigga. See what the hell his problem is."

When Danny didn't respond to what Jamir said, Jamir stood. He felt like someone was stirring up some bullshit, and he could almost bet that it was Danny who held the spoon.

"Go 'head, D. Call that mufucka up. Tell him I want a sit down, just me and him. If he can't make it, then the whole deal is off."

"A'ight, I'ma call him up and see what he got to say. But once that nigga's mind is made up, that's it, so don't expect him to change up too much."

"Well, I'm pretty good at convincing people to get on my level, so don't count me out."

Danny shook his head and pulled out his cell phone. He noticed that he had a missed text from Missy and quickly deleted it without reading what it said, just in case he had to pass his phone to Jamir. He dialed up the number Timbo had given him, and he answered on the first ring.

"Fuck you calling me for? We already discussed what we needed to discuss, so you must have something real important to tell me. I got shit to do so get to talking or I'ma hang up."

"Yo, I talked to my boy and he ain't smiling about your numbers. He say he wants to sit down and talk, try to change some things up. How you feel about that?"

"What the hell you mean, how do I feel? What I said is what it is. But if he feeling like he can change that, he gonna have to wait a few days because I had to leave town. If he can't wait, he can make that trip to my territory. Maybe he can watch and see how a real nigga gets down. I'd like to hear what the lil nigga got to say. So what it is, playa?"

"I'll talk to him and let you know."

"You do that, and make sure you get back at me."

Danny pressed end on his cell phone and looked up at Jamir, who stood in the kitchen doorway waiting to hear what the deal was. As bad as Danny wanted to make up a lie, he couldn't think of what to say, so he decided to just go with the truth.

"Aye, that talk is gonna have to wait. Timbo had to pull back up in the DMV, so he ain't available."

"What you mean wait? I need a re-up, and I ain't trying to put that shit off no longer."

"Sorry, bruh, but what other option do you have?"

"I say we go to him. Call that mufucka back and tell him we coming up."

When Danny didn't pick up his cell phone, Jamir looked at him crazy because he didn't seem too eager to call Timbo back. Jamir felt like some funny shit was going on, but he wasn't about to let it stop him from handling what he needed to handle. If it was too much for Danny, he needed to let him know because Jamir was ready to make a move.

"The fuck you keep hesitating for? You 'bout to have me feeling some type of way. Call his ass back. Tell him we can make that trip to him."

"A'ight. Damn, nigga, just calm down. I'll take care of it."

Danny finally dialed Timbo's number again and, just as before, he answered on the first ring. Jamir listened as Danny told Timbo that they would be going to him. Once satisfied, Jamir walked out of the kitchen. Danny wasn't too sure about the move, but he didn't want anyone to know it. He didn't have no other choice but to go along with things. He had to make sure Jamir didn't mention the first price that he had given him, because he couldn't afford to be exposed, especially in front of Timbo. So when Jamir walked back into the kitchen with a bag, Danny gave him his take on things.

"Yo, Mir, I don't think you should mention only numbers to him. Go in and tell him what you about and then wait to see what he throws out at you. See how low you can get him to go."

"Oh yeah? And why do you feel like that will work? The way you talking, it seems to me like you already know what's up. You sure worried about them numbers. Make me feel like you ain't deliver that message from him right."

"Nigga, you tripping for real. We been doing this too long together for me to try you like that. I'm solid, and you know all my loyalty lies on this side."

Jamir stared at Danny with a skeptical look on his face. He had never trusted him, or anybody else, for that matter. He had let his guard down and given his old connect, Malcolm, the benefit of the doubt, and still got fucked in the end, although Malcolm had done it unknowingly. Jamir was sure that he would find some type of flaw in Danny's story, but the only way to find out was to talk to the head man himself. He was sure that Timbo would love to put Danny out there, and when he did, Jamir would keep it to himself and use the information at a later time.

"Hah, D, I'm just fucking with you. I know you got my back. You've always had it, and I know you always will. I'm grateful to have someone loyal as you on my side."

"Thanks, Jamir. You know I would never lead you into a fire. You my nigga, and I always got your best interest at heart."

Jamir smiled at the comment and gave Danny some dap. The two of them decided to call it a night and would meet up the next morning to make the drive to the DMV, better known as the D.C., Maryland, and Virginia district. Jamir hoped things went according to plan. If so, he would be back on his grind by the weekend, and he couldn't wait to hit the streets.

Chapter 8

Jamir woke from the deep slumber he had fallen into. He was pissed because he had tossed and turned for hours before he finally fell asleep. He could usually just lie down and be out, as soon as his head hit the pillow. But lately, so much had been going on in his mind. It was shit that he just didn't want to deal with, but knew that one day he would have to. Jamir wasn't a little boy anymore, but he still felt like he was too young to have so much drama in his life.

He wondered if Malcolm would ever try to reach out to him again. If he did, Jamir wasn't sure how he would react. Rachel wasn't his bitch and she had probably slept with half the niggas on the block, but fucking his connect hit a little too close to home. He didn't understand why she had such an effect on him. As hard as he tried to move past her indiscretion, he just couldn't do it. The thought of her alone made his dick jump. He had to admit, she was a beast in the bed. He had never fucked a bitch that made him feel the way she did. His mind made him believe that he never wanted to see her again, but his heart told him that he already missed her.

Jamir finally threw the covers off of his boxer clad body and sat up. He swung his legs over the side of the bed, and then picked his jeans up from the chair. He reached in the front pocket and pulled out the small baggie of cocaine. He felt like the white powder would help ease some of the tension, but knew it would only be temporary. Once the numbness wore off, it would be back to square one, so he decided to not even waste the time. He pushed the package back in the pocket and placed the jeans beside him. He wouldn't be able to fall back asleep, so instead, he stood and went to the bathroom so he could take a piss.

After he washed his hands and walked back into the bedroom, he heard a light knock at his window. The digital alarm clock on the nightstand said two-thirty. He couldn't think of anyone who was bold enough to knock on his window, or even his door, at that time of morning. But someone had, and he was about to curse they ass out. Jamir leaned over and pulled the curtain slightly to the side. The eyes that stared back at him made him anxious and mad all at the same time. He didn't know how to react to her presence, but he couldn't just let her stand out there. He shut the curtain, walked to the back door and opened it, so she could enter, even though, she looked terrified to do so.

"The fuck you want? Shouldn't you be somewhere sucking a dick? Or have you reached your quota for the night?"

"That's not fair, Jamir, but I'll take it. I didn't know that he was your connect, and I'm sorry. How long are you gonna hold it against me?"

"What is it that you want, Rachel? I got a road trip to make in the morning, so I need to rest up. Speaking of trips, I thought you was leaving town. Why you still around?"

"I am leaving, Jamir. I get on a bus at ten, but I needed to see you one more time before I did."

"A'ight, well you saw me, so take your ass on, and do what you need to do for you. I'm good."

"Jamir, I might get high and fuck around from time to time, but I do have feelings. I can't stop myself from having love for you, so you just have to understand that it's not going anywhere."

"A nigga like me don't need your love, so you can give that shit to another mufucka, just like you give 'em the pussy.

77

That shit you giving don't belong to me, so you don't owe me a damn thing. Save your explanations and regrets for the next man you lay down with 'cause I don't wanna hear them."

Rachel didn't respond to his comment. Instead, she pursed her lips together and nodded her head. She wasn't sure what else she could say to him, so she counted her losses and walked back out the door. When it slammed shut behind her, she flinched. All she could think to do was get on that bus and leave. She wanted to get herself together so she could be the type of woman Jamir needed in his life. Starting over would be hard because she had been on the pipe for so long. But to gain Jamir's love and affection, she was willing to do anything.

Jamir stood with his back to the door. He hated to shut Rachel out, but what other choice did he have? She wasn't someone he could build a life with. He needed someone that could hold him down when shit wasn't right, but he couldn't think of anyone who could hold that position. Even if Rachel did clean up and get off the pipe, how could he be with her? He wouldn't be able to sleep at night without wondering if she was getting high every time she went out. He just wouldn't live like that.

"Fuck that bitch. I got more important shit to think about."

Jamir turned around and locked his door and then picked up his jeans so he could pull the cocaine he had stashed in them back out. He needed something to block the thoughts of her and felt like a couple of lines would do the trick. But no sooner than he had them laid out, another knock sounded at his back door. Thinking it was Rachel coming back, he didn't bother to put the cocaine to the side. She knew of his habit, so why try to hide it. Jamir undid the locks and pulled the door open hard. He was going to curse her out and ask her what her problem was. He didn't want to be fucked up with her, and he was determined to make her understand that.

"The fuck is you knocking at my door again for? Didn't I just tell you that I ain't wanna hear none of that bullshit you spitting? What the hell is wrong with you?"

"Hold up, nigga. Who the hell is you talking to? You either done lost your damn mind or you was expecting someone else. Which one is it?"

"Sorry, D, I thought that fiend that just left from here, knocking on my door, had the nerve to come back. You know them mufuckas always be coming with those lame ass excuses of why they need some credit. I ain't got time to be catering to those suckas. But what's up with you though? The fuck is you doing here so damn early? Do you even know what time it is? We agreed we wasn't getting on the road until after lunch, so what's going on?"

"Bruh, I tried to lay back and chill, but you know I can't get any rest at home. Trish ass stay with that bullshit. I'm telling you, Jamir, I'm about ready to off that bitch, just so I can get some peace. It done got old. I don't understand why she can't just relax and enjoy the life I'm giving her. She ain't got to lift a finger and do nothing but take care of our son. I pay for everything, but it seems like that ain't even enough."

"You got to give bitches like that more of your time. They get lonely when you be out in the streets so much. Pussy start aching and shit. Hell, stay in one night and blow her fucking back out. I betcha she'll act right after that."

"Yeah, that sounds all good, but I can't do it, my nigga. I don't know what it is, but she don't even turn me on anymore. Dick take forever to get hard when I'm with her. It used to stand at attention just from the sound of her voice, but now that mufucka be limp. I only stick around because of my son."

"Damn, D, I ain't know all that. I don't know what else to tell you. I keep my shit strapped up because I ain't about to let a bitch tie me down like that."

"Yeah, whatever, Mir. Anyway, I'm tired as hell and just wanna lie down and get a couple of hours sleep. You mind if I crash on your couch?"

"You good, but don't make that shit no habit because I don't spend the night with niggas."

"Uh-huh, that ain't what the block say."

"Nigga, fuck you. I'm going back to bed."

Danny laughed and started to walk away, but paused when he saw the plate on the dresser. The two lines of white powder were perfectly straight, as if they were just there for display. He gave Jamir a funny look because he wasn't sure if it was laid out for him or someone else. Danny felt like the only way to find out was to ask, so that's what he did.

"Mir, you got company or is that for you?"

Jamir played it cool and thought about his answer. He didn't want Danny to know about his little habit because he felt like he would use it against him one day. He thought that Danny was a little more naïve than other niggas, so he told him a quick lie.

"I ain't gonna lie, I was expecting that hoe Erica to show up and break me off. Heard she liked to butter her nose, so I set up a couple of lines to get her started. I ended up falling asleep waiting on that bitch, and she had the nerve to not even show, but I'ma put a foot in her ass when I see her. That shit was flaw as fuck."

"Nigga, you gonna need more than a couple of lines for that bitch. Hoe on that pipe. She tried to make me give her a fifty piece just for some head. I told that bitch I'll jack my shit first and sent her on her way. Ain't fucked with her since."

"So you mean to tell me that you passed up some head?"

"Hell yeah. Why would I give a hoe a fifty when I know for a fact that I can get my shit sucked and then get in the pussy for a dime? I'd have to be the dumbest mufucka on earth to do that."

"You got a point there. I guess I'ma just bag that shit back up and go to bed. I need some sleep to make that drive."

"Deuces, my nigga, I'm out, too. Have a good night."

As soon as Danny walked away, Jamir hurried and put the cocaine back in the baggie. As bad as he wanted to snort the lines, they would just have to wait until another time. He finally laid back down, but when he closed his eyes, Rachel came back to his mind. He needed to figure out a way to shake her, but couldn't think of anything that would work. Even fucking Erica didn't help like he thought it would.

***

When Jamir opened his eyes, he hadn't even remembered going to sleep. His early morning hard-on made him want to stay in bed. But he had business to tend to and his money was more important than a quick nut. He heard someone moving around in the kitchen and remembered that Danny had spent the night. He got up to see what was going on because he could have sworn he heard a female's voice, too.

Jamir walked into the kitchen and paid close attention to the interaction between his sister and Danny. He wasn't sure what Missy was even doing there in the first place, but she seemed to be a little too comfortable with his company. They had been so in tune with each other that they didn't notice him until he spoke.

"Y'all mufuckas seem mighty comfortable together. Someone wanna enlighten me?"

"Oh, Jamir, come on, big brother. Get the dick outta your ass. We're just in here talking and having fun, ain't shit else going on, so lighten the hell up."

Jamir was thrown off by the way Missy talked to him. She had always showed him respect, so it threw him completely off. He understood that she was no longer a little girl. When he found out that she had started fucking at fourteen, he fought the urge to murder the mufucka that took her innocence. He wasn't sure what he would do when she no longer needed him, but he'd be damned if she didn't respect him.

"Since when did you feel like it was okay to talk to me like I'm some random ass nigga? Grandma raised you to always be a lady, but I'm starting to see signs of a hood rat. Is that who you are now? If so, just let me know, and I'll treat you as such."

"I'm sorry, Jamir, I ain't mean no disrespect. I was just playing around. You always be so serious and I just wanted to make you laugh."

"Yeah, well it didn't work. Why you here anyway? Me and Danny got shit to do, and I don't need you involved."

"Enough said, big brother. I'm leaving, but one day you're going to make me leave and I ain't ever gonna come back."

Missy stormed out of the kitchen without another word. Jamir kept quiet until he heard the sound of her car engine. When he knew she was gone, he turned around to walk out of the kitchen, too, but left Danny with some parting words.

"Keep playing, nigga, and she gonna be the death of you."

Danny said nothing in return because he couldn't find the words. He knew that Jamir was serious, and he planned to talk to Missy when they got back to tell her they would chill for a while. Jamir was a smart nigga, and Danny needed him in his corner, so no matter what Missy said, he was backing off. Danny wasn't into her like that anyway. He just liked the free fuck whenever he could get it, but he knew he could get his dick wet anywhere. The sound of Jamir walking back in the kitchen broke Danny from his thoughts.

"Aye, bruh, you ready to hit the road? I'm trying to get there, handle business and get back. You down?"

"Yeah, Mir. I'm ready, but we need to have a talk about that shit you said."

Danny had grown tired of Jamir acting like he was a big boss mufucka. He wasn't one of his minions and had grown tired of being treated as such. Danny knew money changed niggas, but he didn't feel like Jamir's money was big enough to inflate his ego, unless he had missed something along the way. He didn't have time to sit and dwell on it, so he got up and went outside so he could wait on Jamir to finish getting his shit together. Danny hadn't told Trish that he would be gone for a couple of days, so he knew there would be hell to pay when he returned. Danny was lost in thought when Jamir walked up on him.

"Your ass better not be daydreaming about my sister."

"Fuck you, nigga, it's your momma I can't get off my mind. Bitch kept me up all night."

"Ya know, I would believe you but your dick don't even stay hard that long."

Danny shook his head and got in the passenger's seat of Jamir's car. He hated that mufuckas knew about his two-minute performances and vowed that the next time he fucked a bitch, he would pop a Viagra pill and give them something they could really talk about. In the meantime, he would sit back and enjoy the ride.

***

Jamir pushed on Danny's shoulder and caused him to wake up. He knew how to get to the heart of the DMV, but that was it, so he needed Danny to point him in the right direction. Once Danny realized where they were, he put in a call to Timbo, letting him know they were ready to meet up. Once they were given directions, Jamir put the car back in drive and pulled off.

It was dark out, but the property brought things to light. Jamir pulled in front of the gate and pushed the button on the small call box. He waited, but got no response from the box. He was about to push the button again, but before he could, the gate opened. He looked to Danny, who in turn raised his brows in wonder. Jamir shrugged his shoulders and pushed down on the gas so he could enter the grounds. The gate shut behind him and he felt like hundreds of eyes were watching him. He knew there had to be a camera system, but it was hidden so good he couldn't see it.

Jamir drove down the small, paved road. He counted the bronze lion statues that lined the sides. The lawn was immaculate, the deepest green he had ever seen. Finally, more lights came in to view and he had to veer to the right to keep from hitting the enormous fountain that sat encircled in the middle of the road. The water that flowed from the marble stone looked as if it was full of sparkling diamonds. Jamir couldn't remember ever seeing anything so beautiful before. He drove around the fountain slowly, just so he could stare at it a little longer. Once he drove the half circle around it, a house that sat a little further down the road came into view. Jamir drove until he saw the pearl white Rolls Royce. He pulled up and parked beside it. He pretended as if it had no effect on him, but he had to admit to himself that he was a little envious. Jamir sat and stared in awe until Danny's voice brought him back to reality.

"Don't sweat that shit, Mir. We gonna be sitting like that one day. Shit, we ain't even twenty-one yet, and we already doing alright. It probably took that mufucka half his life to make enough just to gas that baby up. We already on our way. Just be patient, bruh. We'll be there soon."

"You sure using a lot of we's but yet, you ain't been putting a damn thing in the pot. You only been stirring the mufucka. You should really check your vocab so you speak about shit correctly."

"You know what, Mir? You and I been partners a long time. We used to be equal in this, but ever since your pockets have gotten a little heavier, you been acting like you above me. What's up with that? We supposed to be a team here. Shit, if it wasn't for me, you wouldn't even be parked beside a Rolls right now."

"Nah, D, you got it all wrong. If it wasn't for you, I'd be driving one. You talk about we a team, but I been putting my money up since I was a jit. I've been the one investing in the game, while all you been investing in is some pussy. You so quick to give your shit to the first bitch that drop they panties. You just got your priorities fucked up. I'ma break your ass off for the hook up, but other than that, I don't owe you a damn thing."

Danny was shocked at the words Jamir spat at him, but before he could respond, a knock came at the driver's side window and startled both of them. They both averted their attention to the window and saw Bryan as he stood in the shadows of the house lights, looking like the killer he had been known to be. Jamir nodded and pushed the button to allow the window to lower.

"Y'all niggas having some problems in there or y'all gonna step out and handle what you came here for? Timbo ain't the type of man that likes to be kept waiting."

Jamir nodded once more and pushed the button again, so the window would go back up. He looked to Danny, and then the two of them exited the vehicle. They both understood that their issues would have to be put aside because more important things needed to be handled. As soon as Jamir shut his door, he extended a hand to Bryan, who in turn only stared at him. Jamir pulled his hand back and was about to ask a question, but the soft voice of a female stopped him.

"Excuse me, Tim said that he would not wait all night. If you have business, I do suggest you come inside."

Jamir turned toward the sound of the foreign accent and locked eyes with Nadia. He could tell that she was young, maybe not as young as him, but too young for a nigga like Timbo. The accent, Jamir guessed, was Russian, but her beauty is what held him hostage. He had gone there to pick up a few kilos, not a woman, and he knew that he should stick to the plan. He felt Danny nudge him, and only then did he break his stare.

"Bruh, you good? That ain't what we came here for. If Timbo saw how you just looked at her, your ass won't get shit."

Bryan noticed the exchange between Nadia and Jamir. He had known for years that Nadia had no feelings for Timbo. She stuck around because he gave her all she desired, but the attraction for him just wasn't there. Bryan knew that Timbo would kill her before he allowed another man to have her, so he would do his best to keep an eye on things.

Jamir and Danny followed behind Nadia and went inside the massive house. Danny admired all the expensive things, while Jamir admired the way Nadia's hips moved from side to side. He imagined the way she would move them while she grinded on his dick. Jamir knew that it was wrong to lust after her, but Timbo didn't mean shit to him. He felt like he didn't owe him any respect, but he would try to give it to him anyway. He finally turned his gaze to the layout of the house, and just like the Rolls Royce, it was immaculate.

The staircase was black with gold and white lining and accented the white tile that adorned the floor. Each tile was outlined in black with sparkling gold pieces etched inside the small squares. Jamir felt like he was walking on expensive glass that would shatter at any moment. He tried to walk as light as he could, even though he knew he was just tripping. Nadia led them to the back of the house and through a set of sliding glass doors that were so clean, they looked to already be open. Danny let out a low whistle when he saw the expansive lawn. It seemed to be acres of green in the backyard, with a pool big enough for an army to swim in. As soon as Nadia got close to it, she stripped and jumped in, without warning. Jamir was about to follow suit just so he could get close to her, but the sound of Timbo's voice behind him stopped him in his tracks.

"Don't pay Nadia any mind, fellas. She does her best work in the nude. Come on and join me for a quick drink."

Timbo walked behind a mini-bar and poured three shots of brown liquor. He held one out to Danny, who took it from him without hesitation. He picked up a second glass and held it out for Jamir to take, who in turn held a hand up and refused. Timbo shrugged and downed the glass along with the one he had poured for himself. He could respect the fact that Jamir didn't mix business with pleasure, but he needed him to be a little more relaxed. Timbo sat the shot glasses back down and decided it was time to handle what Jamir had come for.

"Come with me, Jamir. You and I have some things to discuss, things I feel you will be very pleased with."

Jamir followed as Timbo led him back through the sliding doors and into a huge office with a cherry wood desk in the middle of the room. Timbo walked behind the desk and was about to sit down when he noticed Danny had also followed. He wanted to speak to Jamir alone, in hopes that he could convince him of things that Danny couldn't.

"I do apologize for any misunderstanding, but I would like to speak to Jamir alone. Perhaps, I didn't make myself clear the first time."

"Nah, Timbo, we came here as a team. Besides, I think Jamir would feel a little more comfortable if I stayed. Ain't that right, Mir?"

Jamir looked at Danny crazy because, once again, the "we" word had left his lips. Jamir was the only one putting money in the bag, so he felt like it was only his business to deal with. He knew Danny was going to feel some type of way, but he honestly didn't give a fuck. Jamir needed the hook up, and if he had to diss Danny to get it, then so be it.

"Go 'head and step out, D. I can handle this by myself. Me and Timbo here got a lot to discuss, and it may take a while. Why don't you go take a dip in the pool or something? I'll holla at you when I'm done."

Danny scoffed, but turned around and walked out. The last thing he wanted was for Jamir to be alone with Timbo, but he had been dismissed and wasn't shit he could do about it. He thought about the lie he had told Jamir and hoped it wouldn't be revealed. He knew that karma was a mufucka, and it was something he wasn't prepared for. Danny stepped back out of the sliding doors and watched Nadia as she floated in the pool. Then, suddenly, another thought came to mind. He walked to the side of the pool closest to her, so he could put another plan in motion, one Jamir could truly appreciate.

Chapter 9

Once Danny walked out of the room and left the two men alone, Jamir sat down in a leather chair he had his eye on. It wasn't very comfortable, but he had to remember that he didn't go there to relax. Enough time had already been wasted, so without hesitation, he gave it to Timbo straight up.

"So what's the deal? I came here ready to make some ends meet up, and yet we just been fucking around, using up precious time."

"I like that. A man who is ready to get down to business can always have my attention. I'm guessing that since you are sitting here in front of me, that means you don't like the deal I sent Danny to present. Am I correct?"

"Yeah, you spot on. Danny gave me your numbers, but don't you think thirty-two is a little steep, especially when I'm trying to pull in more than one?"

"Thirty-two, huh? Perhaps, you misunderstood."

"No, I think I understood just fine. Perhaps, you ain't understanding that this would be more than a one-time thing. I'm about my business and I expect whoever I spend my money with to be on that same level. So, with that being said, let's talk some numbers."

Timbo sat back in his chair and pulled out a freshly rolled blunt. He couldn't believe that Jamir had the audacity to act like he was running shit. The young up and comer had a lot of nerve to even come at him like that. The only difference was that he had to work under mufuckas until he could get to where he needed to be. It took Timbo years to be on his own, which caused him to envy Jamir's go out and get it attitude. Timbo thought about the numbers Jamir said Danny gave him and wondered if he was telling the truth. He couldn't understand why he would give him false information, unless he was trying to cut himself in. There was nothing worse than having a snake slithering beside you, and it seemed that Danny was proving to be just that.

"So tell me, what kind of numbers are you looking for?"

"I was thinking twenty-eight a brick."

"Twenty-eight? Have you lost your damn mind? You can't actually believe I would sell you my product for such a low price. If I did that, you would be making way more of a profit than me. What exactly do I gain in the deal?"

"You gain a loyal customer."

"I already have plenty of those, and I can guarantee you that none of them pay that low of a price. The best I can do for you is thirty. You take that or you get up and get the hell out of my house."

"Fine. Then I guess my business here is done. I'll let myself out."

Jamir stood and walked to the door, but before he could reach his hand out to open the door, Timbo stopped him, just like he thought he would, because he needed the deal just as bad as him. The luxury cars, the big house and a Russian bitch sucking his dick at night was expensive. Jamir had done his homework, so he knew about Timbo's gambling issues and his debts. There was no way he was about to let a deal fall through, regardless of how low the numbers dropped.

"Alright, perhaps we could discuss things a little further. You are still young in the game, but you are wise beyond your years. You know how to make major moves, even though you're still in the minor league. I do, however, admire your business sense. But you need to have your eyes wide open because your enemies sit beside you and covet what you own. I can assure that I am not the opposition, and it is not my job to reveal who is. That's for you to figure out. Now, I'm going to give you what you asked for, but in exchange, you will agree to deal with only me, no matter what circumstances may arise."

"I'll agree to that, but only if you keep my supply uncut and ready at all times. And as long as you keep shit one thousand, then I won't have a need to shop elsewhere."

"One question. What happened to whomever your supplier was?"

"Let's just say he dipped in the wrong pool."

"Enough said, now why don't you sit back down so we can complete our business?"

Jamir sat back down in the same leather chair. He was proud of himself for standing up for what he wanted. He thought about Timbo's reacting to the numbers he said Danny had given him. But he would deal with that at another time. He had known him long enough to know that he was a snake. That was why Jamir never trusted him. The only reason he kept him around was because he wanted to give him the benefit of the doubt, but Danny continued to disappoint him.

Once Jamir and Timbo finished their business, they walked back out to the pool area, where they found Danny engaged in conversation with Nadia. Timbo wasn't jealous because Danny didn't have what it took to cater to a bitch like her. On the other hand, he would have to watch her around Jamir. He noticed the look in his eyes when he stared at her and hoped it wouldn't become an issue because he would hate to have to kill the young thug, especially over a whore.

"Yo, D, let's get outta here."

As soon as he said it, he turned around to leave and bumped into Bryan, but Jamir wasn't intimidated by the size of him, like others were. His motto was that the bigger they were, the harder they fell. Mufuckas would have to wake up early to try and pump some fear in his heart. Jamir nodded at Bryan and then stepped to the side to let him pass. He understood that it was his territory, so he would respect that.

"How did it go in there? I don't see no duffle bags, so that must mean shit didn't go as planned."

Jamir knew Danny had only asked questions because he was worried about being exposed, but he didn't have to worry because Jamir would save what he learned for the right time. He wanted Danny to believe that shit was sweet between them, so he acted normal.

"Shit went sweet as a piece of pussy. I got that nigga down to twenty-eight a block."

"Damn, Mir, you got him lower than I expected, but where the shit at? Don't tell me we gotta make this trip again."

"Hell nah, that shit already where it needs to be. Don't worry, D, a nigga like me got you. I recognize your place in my life and you ain't gotta worry because I'ma break you off real proper."

"Yeah, nigga, that's what I'm talking about."

Jamir let his words hang in the air and drove carefully down the highway. He didn't want to give the crackers any reason to pull him over. He was back on his way to the top and didn't need anything to hinder him. He looked over at Danny and thought about the snake move he tried to pull, but Jamir wanted to get his payback when the time was right. It disappointed him that his own people would stab him in the back like that. He couldn't understand why mufuckas just couldn't be loyal and live by the code of the streets. He vowed that he would always keep shit real, no matter who he dealt with.

***

When Jamir pulled up in his front yard, he nudged Danny on the arm to wake him up. He planned on breaking him off and sending him on his way. But first, Jamir had to make sure he didn't reveal his stash spot, so he decided to send Danny to the store to pick up a few things.

"Aye, D, take your tired ass to the store and pick us up some blunts and some wine coolers."

"Wine coolers? Nigga, who the hell gonna drink those? That shit is for the bitches. Real mufuckas push back Old E's and shit. Don't let me find out you been drinking like a pussy."

"Just do what I ask so we can spark one up before I send you back home to Trish. You already know she gonna beat that ass for being gone all night."

"Shit. I'ma need a whole blunt by myself before I go home to her. Maybe I should stay here with you one more night before I go and face that demon."

"Hell no. I'm trying to go find some pussy to lay in. The last thing I need is a mufucka in the next room listening to how I lay it down."

"Yeah, whatever."

Danny finally got out of Jamir's ride and got in his own, so he could go pick up the things he was asked to get. He felt like Jamir was just trying to get rid of him, so he could pull out the stash without him seeing where it was. Danny was cool with that, as long as he got what he had earned for the hookup. He walked in the store and purchased the box of Swisher Sweets, along with a four pack of wine coolers for Jamir, and two Olde English 800's for himself. It had always been his favorite brew and he couldn't wait to pop the tops on them. After he completed the transaction, he got back in his ride and drove back down the hill. As soon as he pulled up in Jamir's driveway, his cell phone buzzed. But when he saw that it was Missy, he sent her straight to voicemail, and then got out. Jamir met him at the front door and told him that he had some company coming over, but Danny wasn't going anywhere until he got his cut.

"A'ight, Mir, I know you trying to chill in something warm, but just let me go 'head and get what I earned, and then I'll be on my way."

"I got you, my man. Here you go."

Jamir handed him a small box that held half a kilo inside, which was actually more than he wanted to give him. However, when Danny opened the box to see how much it was, he was actually pleased with the amount. He passed Jamir the wine coolers and the box of Swisher Sweets, and then turned to leave.

"Thanks, Mir. I'll catch up with you in a couple of days. Holla at me if you need me."

"Yeah, bruh, I'll do that. Be careful driving home and make sure you do something nice for your girl off what you make with that. Maybe she'll stop tripping on your ass if you do."

"Shiiit. A million dollars wouldn't stop that bitch from tripping. But all jokes aside, I'ma take your advice and do something nice for her. Maybe take her out to a nice place for dinner, and then take her home and give her this dick for dessert."

"Okay, playa, now you talking. Let me know how that goes."

They gave each other some dap, and then Danny got back in his ride. But instead of going home, like Jamir told him, he texted Missy. He told her to secure them a room at the Holiday Inn, and that he had a special treat for her that night, just a little something that would make her feel good. He smiled at the thought as he pulled into the parking lot of the hotel. He saw Missy's ride and parked beside it. When he got out, she greeted him with the room key dangling in her hand. Missy stayed ready for the dick. He liked the fact that she really didn't care how long he lasted, as long as they were both satisfied.

"Where did you leave my brother at?"

"Don't worry about him baby. He at the house doing his own thing, and he thinks I went home."

"Oh yea? Well you could always make this pussy your home. You ain't got to never go back to Trish tired ass. I could provide everything you need."

"That shit sound real good to a nigga's ears, but how would we explain it to Jamir?"

"He would just have to understand."

"And what about that other nigga you been fucking around with?"

"I cut his lame ass off. Besides, he don't make me feel as good as you. Dick game was whack as hell."

"Whatever you say. Now come on, let's go on up in that room and do what we do best. I got a little something I want you to try."

Danny draped his arm around her shoulders and together they walked to the room that Missy had secured for them. From the outside looking in, you would think they were a solid couple because of the smile each had on their face. When they walked inside the room, Missy wasted no time at all. She turned to face Danny and unzipped his Roc-a-Wear jeans. But he had other things in mind, so he pushed her hand away from him.

"Slow down, ma, you gonna have this dick in a minute. It ain't going nowhere. Go 'head and take off that shit you got on, while I hook a little something up for you."

Missy did just like he told her and stripped off all her clothes. She loved being in the nude around Danny because it made him look at her with a deep lust in his eyes, a lust so real, it almost looked as if he was high. He knew how to make her feel sexy and wanted. It wasn't until she was completely naked that she realized how cold it was in the small room. When she reached to turn the air off, Danny stopped her.

"Leave that shit on, ma, because when you try this pure that I got here, your ass is going to be sweating."

"Uh-uh, Danny, I ain't about to put that shit up my nose. You know I don't get down like that."

"Somehow, I already knew that's what you were going to say, but you ain't even gotta worry. I'ma cook a little bit up so you can smoke it."

"I'm not smoking a damn thing. Don't you remember that my daddy was a crackhead? I am not about to go out like he did. Besides, Jamir would kill me if he ever found out."

"Why you always so worried about Jamir? You ain't a little girl no more, so when you gonna stop letting that nigga dictate your moves? That shit is starting to turn me off. You know what? How about I just take my stash and go find me a grown woman, one who ain't gotta answer to another mufucka."

Danny already knew that the threat of him leaving and going to another female would cause Missy to change her mind. True enough, he didn't want Jamir to ever find out he was fucking her, but he wanted Missy to be free to do what he wanted. He didn't need a bitch in his life that was always worried about the next nigga, even if the nigga was her own brother.

"Wait, Danny. Please don't leave. I'll try whatever it is you want. I'm sure doing it just one time won't hurt me."

"That's my girl, and you should know by now that I ain't ever gonna give you anything that will bring you harm. Besides, you ain't doing it by yourself. I'ma do it with you, so chill out, ma. Just trust me."

Missy smiled at him through her nervousness and then sat on the bed to wait on his next instructions. She watched closely as he pulled a small black bag out of his pocket and emptied its contents on the table. Her eyes grew big from curiosity when he picked up the spoon and poured a small amount of water from his water bottle into its wedge. He added a pinch of cocaine and a dab of baking soda, which he'd had stashed in saran wrap in the bag. When Danny held a lighter under the spoon and heated its contents, Missy was amazed at how the two different powders formed. The white of the cocaine mixed with baking soda turned a light beige color, just from the heat. She had heard stories of how to cook up crack, but she had never really seen it done. It was like some type of magic being performed in front of her, and she wondered if that was how her father had done it. Then, she suddenly began to have second thoughts.

"Um, Danny. You know what? I'm not really sure about this. I don't think it's a good idea."

"I'll tell you what. How about you just give it a try. If you don't like it, I'll never bring it around you again."

"Okay. Just this once."

Danny honestly wasn't trying to listen to the bullshit Missy was talking about. He had been wanting to try the drugs he was pushing but had only settled for it in his blunts. They were no longer getting him high, though, so he wanted to try it another way, in hopes of reaching where he wanted to be at. What better way than to do it and then get a good nut afterwards. He pulled a ready-made glass stem from one of the thick braids in his hair and put a piece of the drug on the wire that was pushed inside. He melted it a little and then held it out for Missy to take but she still hesitated.

"Why I got to go first? I might feel a little more comfortable if you went and then I can go after you."

"Now you know a gentleman, like me, thinks it should always be ladies first. Come on, baby, just imagine it as my dick between your lips and suck on it. I'ma even hold the lighter for you."

Missy reached out and carefully took the stem from him. It was long and slim, but it felt huge in her hand. She looked at it one good time, and then put it between her lips. Then she looked up at Danny. He stood above her and looked back at her with a smile, just to reassure her, and then she struck the lighter and changed her life forever.

Chapter 10

Jamir sat at his kitchen table in the dim light and prepared the beakers so he could cook up the product he had purchased from Timbo. He hoped that it stacked up to what he had gotten from Malcolm because he needed to make sure he maintained an upheld his status as a young G. He mixed and stirred and watched as the cocaine turned in to crack, as he thought back to the look on Timbo's face when he'd mentioned thirty-two a key. All he could do was shake his head at the disappointment Danny continued to bring him. He had known for a long time that Danny was on that hoe ass shit. He was always on his dick, trying to carry his nut sack, but Jamir's shit was too heavy for that mufucka to sling it over his shoulders.

Jamir decided that he would try to recruit a couple of the niggas from the block and form his own crew. He was destined to be a boss and knew that he would need some good, loyal workers. He was almost certain that he could pull Raw and her boy, Blount, to work for him, so he went ahead and prepped some packages just for the cause. Once he was done, he cleaned everything up and then took a long shower. He was exhausted and hoped to get some much needed sleep. As soon as his head hit the pillow, he was out.

***

He woke up early the next morning, well rested, and started his day with a short line of the raw cocaine. He had to admit that the shit was potent, and held his nose to try and ease the burning sensation. Once it had subsided, he went in the bathroom and took a quick shower. He wished he would have had a bitch there to take care of his early morning hard on but since he didn't, he pulled a jack move of his own and took care of the issue.

The heavily starched Polo jeans dropped just enough below his waist to make him still look presentable. Those days of dropping them below his ass was over. If he was going to move up and be a boss, he had to look like one, too. His baby blue Polo shirt and baby blue Timbs made him shine even more. He knew that he would turn a couple of heads in his get up, but he wasn't wearing it for the attention, just because it made him feel good. Once Jamir brushed his fade and put a diamond in each ear, he decided that he was ready for the block.

Jamir stored the pre-made packages in his stash spot before he pulled out of his driveway. He drove through the west end at a slow pace, just so he could check out the scene. It was still early, but he noticed a couple of fiends chilling by the park. They looked as if they had been out all night, so he let them be and kept it moving. He decided to drive down by The Y to see if anything was popping off. As soon as he turned the corner, he saw Erica. He honestly didn't feel like fucking with her at that moment, but he needed some information, so he pulled over to the side of the road and rolled his window down.

"Sup, Erica? The hell you doing out so early?"

"Looks like I should be asking you the same thing. Where you coming from? Another bitch's house?"

"Well since I ain't your nigga, that ain't none of your business. However, I do need you to tell me where I can find Raw. I need to holla at her about something."

"What you need to holla at her about? There ain't nothing she can do for you because she likes the same thing you like."

"I know what the hell she likes, and once again, it ain't your business. Now, you gonna tell me where I can find her or not?"

"Maybe, but if I do, what's in it for me?"

"The rest of your life, that's what. So if you don't want to lose that, then I suggest you answer my damn question."

Erica stood on the outside of Jamir's car with her hands perched on her hips and weighed her options. She liked Jamir and wanted to keep him in her good graces, but on the other hand, she didn't know why he was looking for Raw. She had never seen him fuck with her too much and would never forgive herself if she put Raw in a fucked up position. Erica needed to be sure that Jamir wasn't involved in some type of beef with Raw before she gave up her whereabouts.

"How I know you ain't got some type of beef with her? I would feel like shit if I took you to her and something foul happens. I don't need that on my conscience."

"Look, Erica, I respect that, but I'm just trying to see her about some business. I don't have time for all that beefing bullshit, and I ain't trying to make no damn enemies. I know that Raw be on top of her game, and I like that. A nigga ain't trying to bring her no harm. I give you my word."

Erica crossed her arms over her chest and stared Jamir directly in the eyes. She didn't think that he was underhanded like a lot of the other niggas in the hood. That was one of the reasons why she admired him so much. She decided to let down her tough girl guard and take Jamir to where Raw was at.

"Okay, Jamir, I'm going to trust you and take you to where she is at. The directions are really crazy so you would never find it on your own. You okay with that?"

"I'm cool. Go ahead and get in, but don't think that something else is going to happen. I ain't got no time for anything else. I got too much other shit to deal with and don't need the drama. You understand?"

"Yes, Jamir, I completely understand. Now turn right."

***

Erica proved to be right because Jamir would have never found the house on his own, not even with directions. The ride was smooth, other than the fact that Erica talked the entire time. Jamir ended up learning a lot about her, and he discovered just how intelligent she was. He had always admired a woman with some sense, but Erica's ghetto ass ways turned him off. He knew she wanted to kick it with him on a different level, but that was something he just wasn't ready for.

"So, this where Raw lay her head, huh? The hell she manage to find a house this far out?" he asked as they pulled up in front of Raw's place.

"She didn't have to *find* it, it belonged to her grandparents. When they passed away, it was left to her. Beats paying rent on something else," Erica remarked.

"Yeah? Well, you sure know a whole hell of a lot about her. What's up? Y'all fucking or something?"

"We chilled a few times, but what is it to you? You ain't my nigga, remember?"

"Whatever. But yo, you just gonna sit there and stare at me or you going to knock on the door?"

"Well, I figured since you the one looking for her, you should get your black ass out and knock. I'll wait here for you."

Erica not wanting to get out made Jamir a little skeptical, but he kept his feelings to himself. There was no way he would leave his keys, so he pulled them out of the ignition and got out. He checked his waistband and made sure that his piece was in place, just in case he had to pull it. Raw hadn't expected him, so he wasn't sure what her reaction would be. Once he ensured that he was ready to pop off, he walked to the door and knocked. A few seconds later, he could hear the locks being released. When the door opened, Jamir couldn't believe his eyes.

The honey-colored beauty stood before him in a lace panty and bra set that looked to be too small, but only because of the way they rocked her curves. She smiled and caused his dick to rise. Jamir almost forgot why he was there in the first place, but the sound of Erica's voice behind him made him remember very quickly.

"Hell no. I'll take over from here. Just go ahead and step to the side, Jamir."

Erica walked up and pushed him to the side. Even though she pushed as hard as she could, he barely moved one step. All he could do was shake his head and laugh at the nerve of her. He would let her have that one, but the next one would be on him. He needed Erica to know that she didn't run a damn thing. At that moment though, he needed her, so he decided to let her handle the situation.

"Hi, my name is Erica, and I would appreciate it if you would let Raw know that I am here to see her."

The half-naked female looked Erica up and down with a scowl on her face, and then turned her eyes to Jamir. But before she had a chance to show any type of emotion, Raw walked up behind her in a pair of boxers and a sports bra. Raw put her arms around the female's tiny waist and kissed her on the cheek before she even realized Jamir was at her door. They had never really fucked with each other, so she wondered what had brought him there.

"Sup, Jamir, what brings you my way? Guess I don't have to ask how you found me. What's up, Erica?"

Instead of a response, Erica just rolled her eyes and stepped to the side so Jamir could speak his peace. As she watched him go into business mode, it turned her on. There was nothing sexier to her than seeing a dope boy in action, and she hoped that he would reward her with some dick for the hook up.

"I need to holla at you on the business tip. You got a few minutes to hear what I got to say?"

"Hell yeah. I always got time to talk about some business. Tomeka, go 'head and keep the bed warm while I holla at Jamir. I won't be long."

Raw slapped her on the ass and nodded. Tomeka smacked her lips, but did as she was told. Then Jamir looked at Erica, and without him saying a word, she knew exactly what to do. It was as if she had been through the same routine before. Once Erica was back in the car and out of earshot, Raw stepped out of the house and onto the porch with Jamir. She couldn't wait to hear what he had to say, and listened closely as he spoke.

"I came here to offer you a spot on my team. I feel like it's time for me to build an army of soldiers, and I want you to be one of them. What do you say?"

"It sound good and all, but you know I don't fuck with Danny like that. You already know that me and ya boy got beef. He okay with me being down with y'all?"

"Maybe you ain't get what I said, but I ain't mention Danny. I'm putting you on my team. He ain't got shit to do with that. I need strong, solid mufuckas, and since you fit the criteria, I brought you the proposition. Now, once again, I'm here to offer you a spot. You want it?"

"Well, since you put it like that, hell yeah, I'm down, but I do got one stipulation. My boy Blount got to be included. Me and him always been a team, and when we rise, we rise together or not at all. That's my nigga, so I can't leave him behind. You gonna be cool with that?"

"Yeah, yeah. I'm real cool on that, but all our business stays between us. Danny ain't got nothing to do with what we got going on, so ain't neither of you got to answer to him. Also, you work for me and only me. I'll make sure you never go without a meal, as long as you keep it loyal."

"Shit, nigga, loyal is my middle name, just holla at me when you ready to make it happen."

"I stay ready. That's why I'm here now."

Jamir opened the small duffle bag he had carried on his shoulder and hooked Raw up with half a key. He wanted to see just how shit would unfold before he put out too much work. He assured Raw that he would go up on the amount of product when he saw that things go as planned. Once his business was done, he got back in his ride and saw that Erica had fallen asleep waiting on him. The fact that she didn't nag him while he was handling his business was impressive because most bitches be trying to rush a nigga. He would reward her greatly for her patience.

"Wake up, big head. I knew your ass wasn't thorough enough to hang in the big leagues."

"Well maybe if I was with a nigga in the big leagues, I wouldn't have been bored enough to fall asleep."

"Just hold on, baby, I'm about to turn in my minor league Timbs. A nigga on the rise, and thanks to you, I'm setting up a little team to rise with me. I do appreciate the hook up."

"Oh yeah, well can I show you my appreciation for trusting that I would lead you right?"

"Depends on how you gonna show it."

Instead of responding with an answer, Erica leaned over the middle console and unzipped Jamir's jeans. When she pulled his manhood out, she went straight to work. Jamir ended up having to pull over to get his nut because he was too afraid that he might run off the road. She sucked the hell out of his dick, but it made him want to dip in some pussy. He wasn't about to fuck her in his car, so he pulled into the Motor Inn. But before he could shut the engine off, Erica said something that fucked up his entire mood.

"Are you going to ever take me somewhere besides these rundown motels? Danny at least takes Missy to the Holiday Inn, and he ain't even ballin' like you."

"Wait a minute. The fuck you just say?"

Erica regretted what she had said almost immediately because Jamir's reaction told her that he had no clue about Danny and Missy. She just happened to stumble upon it one day when she had been minding her own business. She couldn't believe that they had been able to keep it from Jamir. She honestly felt bad for revealing their little secret.

"Nothing, Jamir. Don't pay anything I said no mind. I was just talking shit."

"And you gone be eating shit if you don't tell me what the hell you talking about."

"Okay, damn. I don't know what's going on, and I could be wrong about it, but I saw Missy and Danny last night at the Holiday Inn. At first, I thought it was just a coincidence that both of them were there, but I watched them go in the same room."

"You one hundred percent sure about that?"

"I ain't got no reason to lie and make stuff up. I wasn't aware that you didn't know. Please don't let them know that it was me who told you."

Jamir put his car in reverse and backed out of the parking space he had pulled in to. Pussy was going to have to wait because he had more important shit to handle. He couldn't believe that his sister was fucking Danny behind his back. That made two strikes for Danny and Jamir wasn't sure that he would give him a chance to make it three.

Erica already knew that she had ruined everything, so she kept her mouth shut. He took her back to where he picked her up from and dropped her off. He would handle Danny in his own time, but first, he would go find Missy and find out what was really going on. He didn't know what the hell her problem was, but he was determined to solve it.

Chapter 11

Jamir waited on Missy to show up but thankfully, she took her time, which gave him a minute to calm down. He thought about the consequences he would have to deal with, if Danny became the opposition at that point. Jamir was building a team to take over the hood. But since he had only just begun recruiting niggas, it wasn't solid enough to take on a street beef, so he decided to let the shit ride until the time was right to confront his sister and Danny.

He was about to call Missy and tell her never mind, but before he could press her number on the speed dial, she walked in his front door.

"Ain't I tell your hardheaded ass about knocking? You don't just walk up in a mufuckas' shit like that. How you know I wasn't busy?"

"Because if you were busy with one of your hoes, you never would have called and told me to come over here. I know you better than that, big brother. Now, why am I here?"

"Damn, I can't just call and ask you to come over, just 'cause I want to see you?"

"You've never done it before, so don't act like it's normal behavior. Really, though, why am I here? I got shit to do, Jamir."

"Oh yeah? What you got to do that's so important you would diss your brother? I thought you liked chilling over here. What's up with that?"

"I don't have to tell you everything, but since you so damn nosy, I met someone I think I really like, and I'm going to chill with him."

"You met someone? I thought you already had a nigga?"

"Well, I did, but things just didn't work out with us. He was too clingy, and I like my space."

"So what's the nigga's name? Do I know him?"

No, Jamir, you don't know him. Why you asking so many questions? I don't be asking you about your hoes."

"That's because I don't have any for you ask about."

"Well, that ain't what the block says. To hear them tell it, you got all types of hoes sweating you, including crackheads."

"Yeah? Well you tell the block, and whoever them is, that they can suck my dick."

"You sure that's what you want me to tell them? Mess around and they going to be knocking on your door. I'm telling you, Jamir, you are what's happening."

"Go 'head on with that shit, Missy. Matter fact, didn't you say you had someone to go meet up with?"

"Yeah. I'm going, since you done with your interrogation."

"I just be looking out for you, sis. Niggas out there are ruthless, even those you feel like you know. I got the feeling that I'ma have to kill a mufucka over you, so make sure you choose wisely."

"Will do. I'm going now, but I do love you, Jamir, and thanks for caring about me so much."

Jamir leaned down and hugged Missy before she turned around and walked out the door. He wondered if the new dude she was talking about was Danny. He wanted to be one hundred percent sure before he interfered in what they supposedly had going on. He had other things he needed to deal with, like getting his coke cooked up so he could push it out on the block. He went in the kitchen, pulled out all his supplies and got to work. Jamir spent the rest of the night cooking, cutting and weighing his product. By the time he was done, it was too late to do anything else. And he had to admit, his ass was too tired to even think about a dollar.

***

Jamir woke up the next morning with a clear mind. He took a shower, and then made himself some breakfast before getting dressed. It was Friday, and he decided he would hit the block for a few hours and see what was happening. He hadn't heard from Danny since he gave him the half a kilo and wondered what he was up to. So he picked up his cell and dialed his number. When it went to voicemail, Jamir dialed it again, just to make sure that he wasn't tripping. Once again, it went to voicemail. He figured that Danny was probably with Trish, or another bitch, and didn't want to be bothered, so he would wait and try again later.

Before Jamir walked out the door, he laid out two lines of the product he had gotten from Timbo. He hoped the dope was all Danny said it would be because he had already invested his hard-earned cash into it. He snorted one line into each nostril and held his head back. The rush began immediately, and took him to another zone. He relaxed for a few minutes and then gathered what he needed and hit the block. He pulled up on the side of old man Nate's store and parked. He made sure he could see everything from his position, and then got out.

The fiends were out thick, and the money began to flow immediately. For the next few hours, Jamir sat and filled his pockets. The police presence wasn't that heavy, which made it easier for him to handle his business. He enjoyed the nights that flowed with ease, and often wished that there were more of them.

Jamir looked up the block a ways and saw that Raw and Blount were doing their thing. He knew that he had picked the right people to deal his product because neither one of them fucked off when it came time to handle business. Raw had always been low key with her shit, even when she was faced with drama. That was one of the main things he respected about her. Most of the niggas around the way hated on her because she was so smooth. They would always catch their bitches jocking her style, but she didn't pay any of them no mind because she refused to let anything slow her down. Raw was able to let shit go, even when the opps couldn't, and that included Danny. He had been holding a grudge against her for as long as Jamir could remember. That was why Jamir had chosen her to be on his team. Danny would never guess that Raw was in deeper than him, but someone had to be because Jamir had already tested Danny's loyalty, and he had failed.

Jamir was about to pick up his cell and dial Danny's number again, when he suddenly pulled up. He put his phone back in his pocket, and then adjusted his weapon. He could no longer predict what type of bullshit Danny would be on, so he had to stay cautious. When Danny emerged from his vehicle, he was high off something, and Jamir wondered if it was the product he had given him. He didn't want to speculate, so he decided that he wouldn't even ask.

"What's up, Mir? My nigga, how long you been out on the block? I mean, you look like you just stepped out. Still all fresh and shit."

"Well if you would have answered your phone, you woulda known how long I been out here. The fuck you been at, playa?"

"I took your advice and chilled with my bitch for a minute. Cut the phone off and everything. Took her out to dinner, spent a knot on her, and then fucked her real good. Got her ass acting like a lady now, so thanks for the advice."

"No problem. I told you they just want some time. Give 'em that and shit be smooth."

"Yeah, well when you gone settle down and take your own advice?"

"A nigga too young to settle down. Besides, I ain't the one with a child to think about. Don't forget that."

"Whatever bruh, but check this, look like that bitch, Raw, and her partner down the road doing they thang. The money they making should be going in our pockets."

"And why is that? There's enough money out here for everybody. Ain't no sense in being greedy. That shit is what gets a mufucka popped. Don't you know anything about the seven deadly sins? Nigga, greed will get you taken out real quick."

"Oh, so now your ass done turned into a preacher?"

"Nah D, I'm just saying, as long as it ain't starving us, why not let the next man eat too?"

"Yeah, whatever, but I'm telling you right now that one day, I'ma take that bitch out of this world."

"And why is that? You mad 'cause she got a bigger dick than you, or because she can hang longer?"

"Fuck you, Jamir. You know that bitch tried me."

"No, she didn't try you. The hoe you was fucking did. Raw don't owe you shit. She wasn't the one you was sticking your dick to, so you need to let that shit go. Damn, D, it's been how long, and you still on that level? Move on, bruh, and get on something new."

"Why you all of a sudden give a fuck about Raw? Something I'm missing here?"

"You ain't missing shit but this money. We trying to come up in the game and the last thing we need to do is accumulate enemies. She ain't bother us, so why light a flame that don't need to be lit? Chill out, D, and let's make this bread."

Thankfully, Danny listened and let the subject go. The rest of the night went just like Jamir had hoped it would. Customers came from all directions, without incident. Jamir didn't leave the block until he had sold everything he had on him. Danny had run out way before him and left so he could go home early. It was strange behavior for him, and Jamir almost followed him, but he felt like eventually, all things that were in the dark would come to the light. He wanted to let things unfold as they should, so he could handle it the right way.

On his way home, he stopped by The Y and scooped up Erica. When she realized he was taking her to his house, instead of a motel, she was ecstatic. She felt like it was progress, and it gave her some hope. As soon as he pulled in his driveway, she started to open her door so she could get out, but Jamir grabbed her wrist and stopped her.

"Don't think 'cause I'm bringing you here that it means more than what it is, and don't ever show up here, unless I invite you. You got that?"

"Damn, Jamir, why you be acting like that with me? I ain't trying to do nothing but show you that I'm down for you."

"Yeah? Well that's all good, but I don't need you to be down for me. I'm better at watching my own back than anyone else, so I'll pass on that. Right now, though, I'm just trying to fuck something with no strings attached. If you ain't okay with that, then let me know and I can take you back across town. I'm sure I can find someone who is okay with that deal. What's it going to be?"

"Uh-uh. You ain't about to take me back so another bitch can fill my spot and get all that good dick. I am perfectly okay with whatever you want me to be okay with."

The fact that Erica would settle being just a fuck was a complete turn off because, to Jamir, that meant she would settle for less in any situation. A weak ass woman was of no use to him, but he figured since he had already gone that far, he might as well go ahead and get him a nut. He quickly regretted even taking Erica to where he laid his head at, but it was too late to make another move. Might as well get his groove on and get it over with. The two of them finally got out of his ride, but when Jamir went to stick his key in the lock, he remembered that he didn't have any condoms. Erica was not a bitch he would go raw dog in, so he turned around and faced her.

"Hold up, I got to go back up the street and pick up some condoms."

"Haven't we been through this before? If you're worried about catching something, I can assure you that his pussy is disease free. Besides, I ain't even been with nobody since you put it in my life."

"Whatever you say, but it ain't a disease I'm worried about. That shit can be treated."

"Oh, I bet you worried about me getting pregnant. Well, I don't understand how that could be a bad thing, but you don't have to worry. I get the depo shot."

"And I still ain't taking that chance. If you still want to hang, I suggest you get back in the car so we can go and get back."

Erica smacked her lips, but got back in the car. She knew the condom issue would be one she wouldn't win, but Jamir was really starting to piss her off and ruin her mood. She thought about just asking him to take her home, but she was too afraid that she would miss out on another opportunity to be with him. Jamir was unpredictable and emotionless, so she had to settle for whatever time she could get with him. Erica knew that Jamir would be big in the dope game one day, and she was trying to secure her a spot beside him. She was willing to do anything to make him see her for more than just a quick piece of pussy, but she didn't realize that she was going about it all wrong. She also didn't know that his heart already belonged to someone else.

Jamir pulled up on the side of the store, instead of the front, because honestly, he didn't want anyone to see him with Erica. He reached in his pocket, pulled out a twenty-dollar bill and tried to hand it to her, but she gave him a look of confusion, as if it was a foreign object, and rolled her neck.

"What am I supposed to do with that?"

"You suppose to take it, go in the store and buy some damn condoms."

"Why do I got to go in there and get them? You're the one that needs them, not me."

"Yeah? Well to hear you tell it, you the one that needs the dick. So if anything is going to happen between us, you going to need those to get it. Now take your ass on."

Erica snatched the bill out of his hand and got out of the car. Her fucked up attitude had made him lose complete interest. Once she was out of sight, he started his ride and backed out. He didn't have time for her shit. Plus, he was already exhausted from the hours he had spent on the block. He knew that the next time she saw him, she would curse him out, but he really didn't give a fuck. Jamir would rather jack his dick than put up with the bullshit Erica was dishing out. He felt like she wouldn't be bold enough to show back up to his house, but if she did, he had something for that ass.

Jamir pulled back into his driveway and got out. He noticed someone sitting on his front porch, but didn't realize who it was until he got closer. There was no way Erica could have beat him back there, and he wasn't expecting anyone else. Surely, Missy wouldn't be over there that late. He walked up the steps that led to his porch and stopped in his tracks when he saw her. He wanted to be angry, but how could he when he had brought it all on himself? Jamir's tough boy demeanor came out when he spoke, but she knew that it was all a front.

"The fuck you keep popping up here for? Don't tell me, you missed the bus?"

"No, Jamir, I only missed you."

"Get the fuck outta here. I got company coming over, and the last person she needs to see here is you."

"Oh, you mean Erica? Don't look so surprised that I know. I saw you bring her here, but I'm curious, why didn't she stay?"

"What? You watching me now?"

"I've always watched you, Jamir, and I could tell from the look on your face that Erica wasn't who you wanted here."

"You don't know shit. I dissed her ass because she had a fucked up attitude and it ruined the moment. Now, I just want to be alone. So if you'll excuse me, I'm going in and going to bed."

"Okay. Do what you need to do, but I'm not leaving here until we are back straight. I don't care if that means that I have to sleep on that chair. I'm not going anywhere."

Jamir looked into Rachel's eyes and knew that she was serious. He didn't want to chance someone seeing her on his front porch, so he opened the front door and nodded for her to go inside. He could feel his conscience as it ate at him for having brought Erica there in the first place. As bad as he wanted to stay mad at Rachel, he couldn't. She was the one female that could break through his walls and find his soft spot, but she was also the one he could never have a future with, no matter how bad he wanted one.

Jamir slammed his front door and caused Rachel to jump, as if it had scared her. He never wanted her to fear him, but after seeing her in that room wearing Malcolm's t-shirt, he wasn't sure he would always be able to keep his composure. He wanted to blow a hole through somebody, just so he could relieve the pressure that had built up in his heart. But since he couldn't do it, he decided to release that pressure on the person who had put it there.

"I got a little something left over so go 'head and take that shit off. A nigga needs to fuck something up real good."

"I don't want your damn dope, Jamir."

"Guess you don't need mine anymore. I mean, Malcolm is the man, and he has an unending supply, so why you standing in front of me wasting my fucking time?"

"Because I'm in love with you, Jamir, and I know I don't deserve you, but I can't walk away from you. I may not be the ideal woman you had planned on spending forever with, but I don't want anybody else. Dammit, Jamir, I wanna get clean and be somebody, and I just need to know that I have your support. You can't keep hiding how you feel. I see it in your eyes, but you're too damn embarrassed to act on it. Stop fighting it. Put your damn dope boy pride to the side and open up."

"You don't know shit about me, so stop thinking that you do. Now, if you done talking, get naked or leave. Your choice."

Rachel wanted to take off all her clothes right there and submit to Jamir's demand, but she needed him to respect her feelings, not push them to the side, as if they didn't matter. She wanted him to let down his guard and stop worrying about what the next man would think about them being together. She vowed that it was her final attempt to get through to him because she was not about to keep begging him to love her. It was becoming too much for her.

"Alright, I guess I'll be leaving then. You said what you had to say, and I completely understood every word. It's been nice, Jamir. Have a good life and promise me that you'll be careful out in them streets."

With no response, Jamir watched as Rachel reached for the door knob. He didn't know if she had finally given up, but he never meant for her to walk away. He needed someone real, someone who appreciated him, even at his worst, and he was about to let that person walk out the door. He didn't know if his decision was the right one, but he had to stop her.

"Wait. Please, Rachel, wait. I know I been tripping on you about that shit with Malcolm, but how the hell was I supposed to react? You had just left me and then you are all of a sudden with my connect, prancing around in his t-shirt and shit, like y'all a mufuckin' couple. How you think that made me feel? I can't even deal with him no more because of you."

"I was wrong, but you dismissed me, like I wasn't shit. I needed someone to comfort me, and he came along. When he approached me, I didn't know who he was. I know that's not a good excuse, but I was so heartbroken by all that stuff you said. Jamir, you have to know that I would give up everything for you. I just want to be in your life, and not as a secret."

"I know how you feel, and as bad as I want you with me, I can't let it happen. At least not now. I'm on the rise in the game, and I can't risk you holding me back because of your addiction. Just settle for what I can give you and let everything else be."

"I don't have an addiction. I get high because I'm lonely. I just want to be loved and the drugs make me feel like I belong to something."

"That shit don't even make no damn sense. Smoking that stuff has your mind all fucked up. Maybe you should look to treatment, if you really want to stop. But I ain't saying it's going to change anything between us. You done been around the block way too many times with niggas I know, and that's just something I can't live with."

Rachel walked up to Jamir and put her arms around him. When he didn't pull away, she closed her eyes and rested her head against his chest. He was it for her and she would do whatever she had to do to get clean and show him that she was worthy of being a part of his life. She looked up and stared into his eyes. She not only could see his passion but could feel it. There was no way she could let him go, and she vowed to not make any more foolish mistakes. Rachel tipped and put her lips to his, and as always, the two of them fell in sync.

Jamir's lovemaking was full of anger, but it was also mixed with the emotions he kept buried deep inside. Rachel could feel his love for her in every stroke, and savored in its glory. She had to figure out how to get inside him. He was so damn stubborn. When he fell asleep beside her, she told herself that she would go and get clean, and then come back and try once more. As much as she loved him, she couldn't keep holding on and chasing a dream that would never come true. She was still young and had so much life to live. The last thing she wanted to do was waste it on somebody who didn't want it.

Instead of waiting for Jamir to wake up, Rachel got out of the bed and got dressed as quietly as she could. She would respect his wishes and not be there when the sun came up, like last time. She carried her shoes in her hand and tiptoed to the door. She opened it as quietly as she could and stepped out into the cool night breeze. When she walked out on the porch, she finally covered her bare feet. She looked back at the door for the last time, and then walked away.

Chapter 12

Jamir woke up the next morning and found Rachel gone. He wondered what time she had left and why she didn't wake him. He was exhausted and didn't want to think about it. As bad as he wanted to roll over and go back to sleep, he knew that he couldn't. He had to get up and handle his business. Jamir had deemed himself a boss in training and needed to go check on his workers. He couldn't afford to let them run out of product because a true boss didn't let his workers go hungry. He had already made plans to pull in a couple more soldiers once he picked up his next supply. He would slowly build his team up, until it became solid and able to defeat the opps. Jamir had worked toward his goal all of his life. Now it was time that the shit paid off.

He put on a Nike sweat suit with matching tennis shoes and headed out the door. When he pulled up in Raw's driveway, he saw Tomeka sitting on the front porch step with a cigarette between her fingers. Her manicured nails were adorned with gems that sparkled in the morning sun. In another situation, he might have flirted and worked himself up on some pussy. But Raw was now one of his people, and that was a line Jamir would never cross. There were certain rules to the game and his integrity wouldn't allow him to violate them. Tomeka stood when he got up to the steps. The shorts and tank top she had on left nothing to the imagination, but Jamir wasn't on that, so he maintained his composure.

118

"Hey, I remember you from the other night. Where that bitch at you had with you?"

"That bitch is exactly where she needs to be."

"Hmm. You looking for Raw?"

"Yeah. She happen to be here? If not, I can come back by when she is."

"She's in the house with Blount. I don't like being involved in the things she has going on so I dismiss myself from it. Can't say nothing about something I don't know about. Right? Besides, I needed a smoke and Raw hates the smell of cigarettes."

"Yeah, me too, so if it's okay, I'ma go ahead and step inside."

Tomeka shrugged her shoulders and sat back down on the steps. If she could have had her way, she would have given up the goods right there. Tomeka was a dicky-dyke. Jamir could tell from the first time he met her that she didn't have any standards, but thankfully, it wasn't his problem. As soon as he stepped up on the porch, the front door opened. Jamir smiled when he saw Raw, and gave her some dap. Her dreads were braided back into four neat rows and bonded at the ends with different colored rubber bands. She stood there, looking just like a nigga. If he didn't know any better, he would have sworn she had a dick between her legs. When she opened the door wider, Jamir stepped inside and followed behind her.

The inside of the house wasn't very impressive, but with a little work, anything was possible. Jamir could tell from the furnishings that it had once belonged to someone older, and it made him think of all the years he had lived with his grandmother. She had done right by him and his sister when their mother abandoned them, and he would forever be grateful. He swore that he would never forgive the woman who birthed him, and to that day, he had stuck to his word. He refused to let thoughts of her penetrate his mind, so he pushed them away and sat down at the kitchen table across from Raw and Blount.

Raw picked up a black bag that had been sitting on the floor beside her and put it in her lap. She unzipped it and reached inside. She pulled out the large stacks of money and sat them on the table with a smile. She knew that she had done well. The fiends liked to deal with her because she always gave them their money's worth. Raw had been dealing dope in the hood ever since she was fifteen, which was also when she came out as gay. She had grown tired of the niggas trying her, so she finally told them that she liked pussy as much as they did. They couldn't do nothing but respect her choice, and the rest was history.

"So I guess shit must have been sweet out there."

"Shit always sweet when I have my hands in it. This is from a half brick. Imagine what I could do with a whole one. I told you I don't fuck off when it comes to business. I handle mine. I go out on the block with purpose, and I don't let shit stand in my way."

"I got to admit, you did your thing. You actually did it better than I expected. I suppose you still got a little something left. Right?"

"Hell nah. When I hit the block, I do it with a goal in mind and I don't leave until I reach it. Me and my boy here, we get out and get it. Don't get us confused with ya partner, Danny. Now that's the nigga fucking off."

"Well, don't forget that he don't even know what we got going, so let's try and keep it that way."

"I don't talk to that fuck nigga. His pussy ass is the one still walking around holding a grudge. Shit, I can't help that his bitch came to me for that action. If he would have been pushing that wood to her right, she wouldn't have come to me in the first place. He can't be mad 'cause my stroke is longer than his."

Jamir and Blount laughed at what Raw had said. The whole neighborhood was familiar with the story of how Danny got dissed by a woman for a woman, and no matter how much time passed since it happened, the whole block still joked about it. However, it had never messed with Danny's flow of pussy. He wasn't no ugly nigga and could pull any bitch he wanted. His only problem was that he just didn't have the stamina to keep them.

It was time to put all jokes to the side and get back down to business. Since Blount had mostly been quiet, he felt like it was his time to stand up and speak his peace. He usually allowed Raw to handle all the front-line action, while he stayed in the background as muscle. Blount had never tried to outshine Raw because she was a female. They made the perfect team, and to Blount, they were equals.

"So when we getting that refresh? We ready to get on back out there and make some more moves, because it's always business with us."

"I like that, and it was one of the main reasons I chose to come this way. Something made me feel like you were going to need a come up and I wanted to be the one to help you out. I did bring a little something else, just in case. Matter fact, I'll go out to the car and get it."

"Well, if you don't mind, I think I'll join you."

Blount stood at the same time Jamir did because he felt like it was his turn to handle things. He wanted Jamir to feel comfortable doing business with both of them. He needed him to see that he and Raw shared the load and that he could rely on either one of them. When Jamir opened the front door and walked outside, Tomeka stood once again from her perch on the steps. She gave Jamir a look of seduction and then rolled her eyes at Blount. She had never cared for him because he felt like she wasn't good enough for Raw, and he exposed that every chance he got.

"Hey, Jamir, don't mind Lassie. That bitch stays in heat."

"Yeah? I kinda noticed that. Ain't no way a mufucka could miss it, but it seems like Raw is okay with it. What's up with that?"

"I don't know, bruh. I catch Tomeka doing shit all the time. When I tell Raw, she just shrugs that shit off and says that the hoe don't mean no harm. Tomeka play like she gay, but I bet ten stacks that if you put a dick in her face, she'll suck the skin off that mufucka."

"She ever tried you?"

"What? That hoe has tried every nigga on the block, including me, but Raw is my people and ain't no way I'ma disrespect the code like that."

"Why Raw still with her if she's that bad? Bitch sound like she off the chain."

"She is, but for some reason, Raw loves that bitch. Maybe she sees something in her that we don't."

"Ya know, it's hard to find niggas these days that live by the code. It's good to know I got one on my team."

"I'ma always keep it real 'cause I don't know any other way to be. Speaking of keeping it real, what's up with you and Erica? Heard you had her on your side when you stepped to Raw."

"Ain't a damn thing up with me and that bitch. I just needed her to show me how to get out here. I'm a nigga who likes a challenge, and she makes shit too easy, just like the one sitting on the steps. I ain't got time to train a dog. Besides, she ain't even got no morals."

Jamir opened his car door and pulled the plastic grocery bag out from under his seat. He usually never rode with his drugs that easy to access, but for some reason, he took a chance. He would have been caught slipping, and vowed that he would never take that chance again. Jamir shut his car door and sat the bag on the hood of his ride and then pulled out the brick of cocaine. The shit he had bought from Timbo turned out to be better quality than anything he had ever gotten from Malcolm. He was actually happy that things turned out the way they did.

"This too much for y'all to handle?"

"Hell nah. We can handle that and some. Shit, we real gangstas out here, not some play-play wanna-be's."

"A'ight then, this is only the beginning of what I have planned. I'm trying to move up the ranks, form my own crew and take shit over. I don't mind sharing the plate and letting everybody eat, as long as shit stays loyal."

"Me and Raw breathe loyalty, just make sure you don't move on and forget us when you get to the top."

"Forget you? Y'all niggas is going with me."

"Hell yea. That shit sounds sweet."

Blount gave Jamir some dap and then got a serious look on his face. Jamir noticed it and became curious as to what was going on. He had to admit, he liked the fact that Blount could go from laughing to being serious all in the same minute.

"Sup with that serious look? You got something else you need to put me up on?"

"I wanted to ask you about Missy. I mean, what's been going on with her?"

"The fuck is you asking about her for? Lil sis is good. But you know she off limits, so why you so worried about her?"

"Don't worry, Jamir, it ain't even like that. I'm asking because I saw her at the trap house on Orange Street. It just seemed strange that she would go there. I mean, I ain't know she got down like that."

"She don't, which means you must be mistaking her for someone else. Missy would never be caught in a place like that."

Blount got quiet for a minute and thought about how he was going to tell Jamir all that he had seen. That was the main reason he had wanted to walk him outside. He didn't really want to put Missy's business out there like that, but what type of nigga would he be if he didn't. He felt like he owed Jamir that loyalty, because if it was his sister, he'd want someone to look out the same way.

"Jamir, I ain't mistaken. It was definitely her. I saw her go up to A.J. and buy something and then she went up in the trap from there."

"Does Raw know about this, too?"

"No, she don't know anything. You know I stay in the background mostly, so I can observe shit that's going on. That's why I walked out here with you, so I could talk to you alone."

"Thanks. I'll look into it. Holla at me when you ready for the re-up. I got to go."

Jamir got in his car and took off without another word. He hoped that there was some type of misunderstanding because he just knew that Missy would never go out like their father. Jamir had shielded her from so much and would never forgive himself if something happened to her. He didn't think she could have started using on her own and wondered who could be so cruel and introduce her to it. There was only one person he could think of that could have convinced her of such a thing. Jamir had seen them getting more comfortable, and after what Erica told him, it was confirmation. Missy would have trusted that person, and they, in turn, betrayed her. Jamir hoped that he was wrong, but his instincts told him that he was right on the money. There was only one way to find out.

Chapter 13

Jamir sat in the driver's seat of his ride and gripped the .44 tightly in his hand. The magazine stayed full and ready to put a nigga on they ass, but he had yet to put a body on it. The weapon had been a gift from Malcolm eight months earlier. He said that without it, a mufucka would feel like they could try you and get away with it. Jamir liked to think that no one would be crazy enough to try him, and then A.J. proved him wrong.

Jamir never wanted to be a killer, but he understood that being a part of the game made you one. Niggas didn't respect boundaries, and Jamir just couldn't sit back and allow someone to disrespect him. The whole hood knew that Missy was off limits, and there were no exceptions. He wondered how she had convinced A.J. to go against the grain, unless he had already had a mind set to do it. He would have to pay for that mistake.

Jamir sat and watched A.J.'s every move. He had thought about staying in the darkness and pulling the trigger from there, but he had never been a coward and wasn't about to start. How would another learn from A.J.'s mistake, if Jamir let off a round and then hid his hand? He needed mufuckas to take him seriously so that it didn't happen again. He also wanted to look A.J. in the eyes, so he could account for his sin before he sent him to hell. He had been cool with A.J. growing up, but he had never considered him a friend, so the loss would not be a devastating one.

Jamir was ready, and just as he was about to get out and handle his business, a knock at his window startled him. He hoped that when he looked up, he didn't lock eyes with an officer. The last thing he needed was to get busted with a weapon. Who would take care of Missy while he sat inside prison gates with double digits? He knew the white man wouldn't spare him. Instead, they would rejoice in ridding the streets of another black man. That was just the way things worked.

When Jamir noticed that it was Malcolm, he cocked his weapon and sent a hollow tip to the chamber. He wondered how his old connect would feel dying by the very gun he had provided. Jamir hadn't spoken to Malcolm since the incident with Rachel, and honestly, he didn't want to hear shit he had to say. But he guessed that he wasn't going anywhere, until he listened to his reasoning. Jamir wasn't about to get out of the ride because he didn't want to be an open target, just in case Malcolm was there for blood, so he nodded his head to the passenger's side, inviting him in. Once inside, Malcolm wasted no time getting to the point.

"I didn't know that that was your bitch in the room that night. You never mentioned one to me."

"Didn't know I had to, but she ain't my bitch. She belongs to everybody."

"Yeah, but everybody don't feel for her the way that you do. And don't deny it, I saw it in your eyes."

"You couldn't have seen it in my eyes because I don't feel shit. Besides, my emotions and feelings died a long time ago."

Malcolm could see the hurt in Jamir's eyes, even in the darkness of the night. He also saw a lot of himself in him. For he, too, had fallen in love with a crackhead and was ashamed to show it. But when she ended up dead on a back street, he regretted it. He didn't want his young protégé to make that same mistake, but until he could get back in his good graces, he would leave the subject alone and focus on another topic.

"Why you got your gun ready to kill A.J.?"

"Why the fuck you think he's my target?"

"Well, that's who you have been sitting here eyeing for the past half hour. Everyone else has come and gone, and he has remained. If he wasn't your target you would have been gone by now. Don't forget, I've been doing this a lot longer than you. Now, you wanna answer my question?"

"That bastard sold dope to my sister. Everyone knows that she is off limits. He can't get away with that disrespect."

"So you just gone off him and everything's alright? Then when she finds another source, you gone off him, too? You just gone keep bodying mufuckas until one day, they body you? I ain't know Missy was on it like that. You talk to her about it?"

"Hell nah, at least not yet. And yeah, I'ma kill any mufucka that thinks they can sell my lil sis dope."

"Jamir, you need to think about the shit you about to stir up. You still semi-fresh in the game and to hear you tell it, you trying to rise to the top. You can't do that from prison or the grave. That nigga out there just doing what drug dealers do. They sell fucking drugs, bruh. You need to get on with Missy on that tip. Find out when she started that bullshit, and who put her on to it. Then you deal with that first."

Jamir had become frustrated with the words Malcolm spoke because he knew that he was right. In a way, he was glad that he had showed up and stopped him, but he was also still pissed at what A.J. had done. He decided to deal with it at another time and in a different way. But he was still curious as to why Malcolm was even there.

"The fuck is you even here for? I thought I told you that I wasn't dealing with you anymore, and ain't shit changed since then."

"I know what you told me, but I'm only here now, trying to look out for your ass. You ain't got to deal with me anymore, but you don't need to be dealing with Timbo either. Since you fresh in, it should be real easy for you to pull out."

"I don't know what you talking about, or even who you are talking about. So get the fuck outta here with that bullshit."

"Look, Jamir, you can play dumb all you want, but listen to me when I tell you that you need to stop dealing with him. You do not want to get caught up in his mess. Timbo is deep in debt with the Colombians, and has been for a minute. Mufucka is lucky that he's still breathing. You see, he has a serious gambling problem and blows outrageous money on bets, money that's not even his. What he don't gamble away goes to that Russian bitch. He knows it's the only thing keeping her there. If she knew the truth, she'd be gone in a second. So if you don't want to be indebted to them mufuckas, too, then I suggest you listen to me and get out while you can."

"Listen to you, huh?"

"Yes. Pull out, Jamir, or help the Colombians figure out who his other source is."

Jamir looked at Malcolm sideways because he felt like he had tried him. He had never been the type of nigga to speak on another man's dealings, but that was exactly what he was being asked to do. To him, it was the same as snitching.

"So, he is getting his supply from another source, but owes his last source some money. You want me to basically gather information, like an informant, and turn on his ass. That nigga your opp or something?"

"Nah, he ain't my enemy, but he ain't my friend either. I happen to have close ties to those same Colombians, and they're good people. They were good to Timbo, gave his ass a lot of breaks, and he still fucked them over."

"How I know that what you telling me is some real shit?"

"I don't have a reason to lie to you. You dealt with me for over a year and never questioned me, so why would you doubt my word now? You in your feelings because of a bitch, but don't let that shit blind you and cause you to miss what's going on. Just so you know, I'm still on your team, even if you ain't on mine."

"Let's say I believe you and help them out. What happens after that?"

"What happens is doors begin to open for you. The things that you have longed for will fall right into your hands, and you'll soar to the top of the chain in no time. That little shit you getting from Timbo will seem like crumbs compared to the rewards the Colombians will give you."

"If the rewards are so nice, what's holding you back from doing it yourself? Don't you want a seat at the throne, too?"

"I'm already on the throne, Jamir, and I wouldn't mind a real nigga sitting up there with me. My status is solid, and I'm very happy where I'm at. Plus, I ain't no greedy mufucka. I want to see you rise to the top because that's exactly where you deserve to be."

"So, what am I supposed to do?"

"It's real simple. Whatever money you have for product, you give it to the Colombians in exchange for the same amount in counterfeit bills. You'll take the fake money to Timbo, and whatever product he gives you, they will double it. They get their money, and you win all the way around the board."

"Hold up, because I ain't understanding this shit. I thought they wanted to find out who his other source is. How am I supposed to get that information?"

"Easy. You fuck his bitch."

"Man, get the fuck outta here. Ain't no way I'm fucking his woman. I live by a code, bruh, and I ain't about to break it. Only flaw ass niggas do that shit."

"Come on, Jamir, I look at you like family. I never would have even picked her up, if I would have known. I'm trying to make that shit up now, so stop coming at me sideways. It's over with, and I can't take it back, so let's move on past it."

Jamir knew that Malcolm was right. He truly believed that he would never have fucked with Rachel if he had known how he felt about her. The problem was that Jamir didn't want anyone to know. He wondered how it was possible to have feelings for someone you were ashamed to be with. He decided to stop thinking about it and push on. Malcolm had been good to him, and he didn't have any reason to believe that he wouldn't continue.

"A'ight, my bad. I'ma stop throwing that shit back up, but don't let it happen again. And don't let nobody know how I feel about her. I don't want to lose the respect of the hood."

"How you feel about that girl is not going to cause you to lose respect from your peers. All they watch for is how you handle your business. You get more respect by keeping shit real, so you should never be ashamed of your feelings. Thugs have hearts, too. You should really think about following yours before you fuck around and miss out on what's in it."

Jamir liked that Malcolm had always been wise in his words, but he couldn't think about what was in his heart, at least not at that moment. He had a new mission in mind, and even pushed the thoughts of killing A.J. to the side. He wasn't too keen on having to fuck the Russian bitch, but he would do whatever he had to do. He just hoped he didn't mess things up.

"How am I supposed to convince the lady to lay down with me?"

"Don't worry, Nadia is easy pussy. Show her that you're interested, and she will make the rest happen."

"You been in it before?"

"Who ain't been in it? All you got to do is show her a wad of cash and she will be down for whatever. That's how Timbo has kept her for so long. He swooped in like a hero and took her from some drastic circumstances. Fed her dick and money, and then he put a ring on it. But even though he did all that, she can't stand him. She finds him desperate and weak. She don't even look at him like a man anymore. It's just more convenient for her to stay there now."

"So what happens if he finds out I'm sticking dick to his beloved? Don't you think that will mess up the whole plan?"

"He won't find out, at least not until it's too late. But Timbo is a pussy himself. If anything, he will get Bryan to handle the indiscretion. But before he even has a chance to move on you, he will be taken care of."

"A'ight, then I'm ready. Let me go 'head and get my money together now. I'll call you with the amount."

"Bet that. And, Jamir, I truly am sorry about ya girl."

Malcolm got out of Jamir's ride and disappeared into the darkness. Jamir sat for a moment and thought about all that he had been through to get to the point he was at now. He looked up and set his eyes on A.J. one more time before starting his car back up and pulling out of his hiding spot. He still wasn't going to let A.J. get away with selling dope to Missy, but he would postpone the mission until another time. He had an even bigger mission to accomplish, and it would make him be recognized for who he really was. A Boss.

Chapter 14

Missy had called Jamir and told him that she was going out of town with one of her friends, but deep inside, he felt like she wasn't being completely honest. He didn't want to give her the benefit of the doubt, but what other choice did he have. He just found it convenient that Danny claimed he had to make a trip to see some old friends at the same time. Jamir knew that he had to accept the fact that Missy was no longer a little girl. He needed to let her go so she could find her own way. Blount confirmed that she hadn't been back around since the night he saw her buy drugs from A.J. Jamir had to believe that the time she was seen buying product was just a misunderstanding. He just didn't think that Missy would go out like that.

He pushed those thoughts out of his mind and concentrated on the matter at hand. His exchanges with Timbo had been going according to plan, but it was time to execute the rest of it. With Missy and Danny both out of his way, it would make things less complicated. Nadia had told him that Timbo would be gone on a run and wouldn't be back for three days, so Jamir was on his way to give her what she had longed for. He had never fucked another man's woman in their home, but he was about to do just that. And for some reason, he felt no guilt.

The Colombians had delivered as promised, so now it was his turn to give them what they needed to shut Timbo completely down. Jamir wondered if doing the job would classify him as a snitch. He knew everything had to be done on the down low, and he was cool with keeping the shit to himself, but he wasn't too sure how Nadia would display things.

When he finally pulled up to Timbo's estate, he let out a sigh of frustration. He hoped that he would only have to fuck her once to get her to reveal the information he was seeking, but he somehow felt like Nadia would draw things out. She seemed like the type of bitch that would play a mufucka at they own game, and Jamir felt like he would be no exception.

Jamir felt a presence and looked up to see Nadia, as she stood in front of his vehicle with nothing on but a lace thong and a pair of gold six-inch heels. She sipped on one of the tall glasses of champagne she held in her slender manicured fingers, while she sat the second glass on his hood. As soon as she drank the sparkling liquid, she sat the empty glass beside the other one and then leaned on the hood. Jamir wasn't sure if he should get out or just sit there and enjoy the show. He had to admit, the bitch had a flawless body, with not an ounce of fat on it. She actually seemed fragile, and Jamir was determined to break her.

Nadia smiled and did the 'come here' motion with her finger. Jamir knew he needed to get out and handle his business, but he was so mesmerized looking at her flesh that it made his movements slow. He could feel his dick grow in anticipation of what was to come and knew that it would all be worth it in the end. He had nothing to lose and so much to gain. So without further ado, he got out and shut the car door behind him. Nadia was a good temptress and he was the prey, but he would soon turn that shit around.

"What's the matter, Jamir, never seen a naked woman before?"

Nadia's Russian accent seemed deeper than before, and he had to take a moment to understand what she had said. He walked up closer to her and took the glass of champagne off the hood, where it still sat. Jamir had never been a drinker so instead of putting the glass to his mouth, he poured it between her breasts and sat the glass back down before he licked the liquid off of her flesh.

"I've seen plenty of naked women, but none as beautiful. I say we go inside so I can see even more of you."

"Why wait until we go inside. You ain't never fucked a bitch on the hood of this ride? This warm hood makes my pussy so wet."

"Oh yeah? Let me be the judge of that."

Jamir slid his hand between her legs and pushed her thong to the side. When he realized how ready she was, he decided to do just what she had asked. He started to pick her up and sit her on the hood, but she stopped him. She needed excitement because she had been bored with Timbo for so long.

"No. I want you to bend me over and fuck me hard. Don't be afraid to get nasty with me, Jamir. I like it like that."

"Oh, that's how Timbo give it to you?"

"Hell no. That bastard's dick has gone boring as hell. All he cares about is gambling. He could care less about my needs anymore, that's why I need a real man to make up for all that I have missed. Can you handle that, or should I seek out someone else?"

"Don't worry, a nigga like me is going to make it feel like you ain't missed a damn thing. I'ma make your whole life have new meaning."

Jamir undid his jeans and pulled a condom from his back pocket. Nadia gave him a disappointed look but there was no way he would push up in her without it. He would pull out of the deal he had made first. He was already taking a chance by fucking her. The last thing he wanted to do was add insult to injury and get her pregnant.

"Do you really need that? You know, I feel like it takes all the fun out of it."

"Well, you another man's bitch, not mine. So yeah, I need this. I'm sure Timbo wouldn't be too happy about me planting seeds in his garden, and something tells me that it's too good to pull out of. So, it's with this on or ain't shit going to happen. Your choice, but it's how I roll."

Nadia shrugged her shoulders and sucked her teeth, then pulled the condom from Jamir's hand. He watched her closely as she tore it open and stuck it on the tip of his dick. She completely blew his mind when she kneeled down and put her mouth over the condom and pushed it the rest of the way on his manhood. He wondered where she had learned the trick from and how many men she had done it to before him. Once the condom was secure, she let him fall from her mouth and stood up. She licked her lips and then pulled the thongs she had on down her long, slender legs before she stepped out of them.

"Okay, you win this time, but I hope you don't make it a habit. You better not disappoint me either."

Jamir nodded and wondered if the comment was a threat or just a bitch talking shit. He hoped, for her sake, that it was the latter.

Nadia turned her back to him and bent over. Jamir spread her wide and pushed into her with no hesitation. The force of him entering her caused her to let out a low grunt that soon turned into a moan. Jamir put a hand on each one of her hips and fucked her hard. He would release all his frustration on her because she didn't mean a damn thing to him. The sounds of their flesh meeting cause a low echo, but thankfully, there was no one to witness it.

It only took Jamir about ten minutes to bust his first nut. He had to admit that the pussy was good, even with a condom between them. He knew that what he was doing was just a job, but he told himself that he wouldn't mind doing some overtime. Nadia turned out to be a straight freak and did things to Jamir that he never could have imagined. She had a high stamina and her pussy stayed wet. No wonder Timbo gave her all he could. By the time Nadia finally came off his dick, he was exhausted. He wasn't even sure that he could drive to the hotel he had secured for himself, because he hadn't planned on spending the night. However, things don't always go as planned.

When Jamir woke up the next morning and found himself still in Timbo's bedroom, he panicked. He remembered that Nadia told him that Timbo would be gone for a few days, but it still didn't relax his mind. He was about to get up and get the hell out of there, but the sound of Nadia's voice stopped him.

"Now you know you can't leave until you've at least had breakfast. I do make a mean omelet."

"Nah, I think I'll pass. I really need to head back home, so I can check on my sister, but thanks for the offer."

"It is really sexy for you to care about your family so much, but maybe I can interest you in something else."

Nadia pushed Jamir back on the bed where his head laid on the same pillow that Timbo slept on. His early morning hard-on stood at attention as Nadia straddled him and made it disappear inside of her. He was so lost in the moment that he almost forgot that he didn't have a condom on. Once he realized it, he pushed her off of him and sat up.

"Uh-uh, nice try, but it's not going to happen. At least not yet. Let me get a feel of things first, and then I'll relax."

"You mean, you didn't feel enough last night? You did bring out the beast in me, and I can assure you that it has been a long time since anyone has been able to unleash that."

"Well, let me see what else I can pull out of you."

Jamir picked his jeans up off the floor and pulled out another condom. He examined the wrapper to make sure it hadn't been compromised, and then tore it open. Once he strapped back up, he spent the rest of the morning deep inside of Nadia. He would let her get a few more orgasms for nothing, but he planned on asking questions the next time they were together. Little did he know, the information he was seeking would not come that easy. Once he began asking questions, Nadia became more reserved. He believed the mission was going to be a bust and voiced his concerns to Malcolm.

"I'm telling you, that bitch ain't giving up a damn thing but some pussy. There has to be another way to find out the information."

"Damn, Jamir, it sounds like you are getting tired of her already. What's the deal?"

"Honestly, bruh, I am getting tired of her ass. I feel like she is trying to trap me. Bitch be trying to make me fuck her without protection. I mean, I actually check my condoms to make sure she ain't poke no holes in them. Am I tripping, or what?"

"That shit is crazy, but you have to pull through on your end of the deal. Come on, you on top of the world right now. Plenty dope, plenty money and a pretty Russian bitch at your service. What more could a man ask for?"

Jamir thought about the question, but had no answer for it. He didn't want to seem ungrateful for all that Malcolm had done for him, but he had grown tired of Nadia very quickly. He began to feel like she knew what he was up to, but he decided to give it one more shot before he gave up.

"Ya know, Nadia, it could be just me and you together in this big ole house. No more sneaking around. We could enjoy all of this and plenty more. I could take over Timbo's business dealings while you lay your pretty ass by the pool after a day of shopping. We could live happily ever after with no worries at all."

"That sounds wonderful, but how do you suppose we do that? Timbo would never allow that to happen."

"What if he didn't have a choice? Just tell me who his connect is, and the rest should fall right in place."

Nadia actually believed in the fairytale that Jamir had sold her. She had dreamed of a happily ever after ever since she was a little girl, she just didn't know that a dream was all it ever would be.

Once Jamir informed Malcolm and the Colombians of the information Nadia had given him, they in turn informed Timbo's source that the money he had been giving them was counterfeit. Once it was verified, they executed Timbo along with Bryan and Nadia.

Danny was stunned at what had happened, but had no idea that Jamir played a big part of it.

"Damn, Mir, that shit that happened with Timbo was crazy."

"Yeah, it was. I'm just glad that neither one of us was there when it went down. That could have just as easily been us. He must have really pissed a mufucka off for them to go at him like that."

"So what happens now? He was my only connection to anything. You going to need somebody."

"Nah, D, a nigga already got that shit worked out."

Danny found it strange that Jamir already had another source. He didn't seem bothered by what had happened to Timbo, even though he had been dealing with him for months.

"Aye, Mir, you don't seem like that shit that happened to Timbo is bothering you. What's up with that?"

"In these streets, you can't ever get close to a mufucka. You don't know when it's going to be your last day, or theirs, so you got to keep your emotions in check. If you don't, they could get the best of you and kill you themselves. Many people think I'm heartless, but I'm not. I just don't let nobody in, so that way, shit like that don't affect me."

What Jamir had said made plenty of sense. In fact, it made all the sense in the world, but Danny still felt some type of way. Timbo had been his people and, although he wasn't very fond of Bryan, he still felt the loss. Jamir, on the other hand, was ready to get back to business. He had plenty of dope and a nice stack of money put to the side. His heart told him to take some of that money and go give it to his grandmother, but he hadn't been to see her in months. He didn't want to have to explain his absence. He was sure that Missy kept her abreast of what was going on, but he stayed away. Jamir was trying to concentrate on his thoughts when Danny interrupted him.

"I say we make a move on Raw and her boy. The mufuckas done came up somehow, but I say we take 'em back down."

"The fuck you mean take them down? How do you suppose we do that?"

"Mask up and run up on them. How else you think we gone do it?"

"Nigga, I'm a lot of things, but a jack boy ain't one of them. The hell I look like running up on the next man? I already told you, I got something lined up, so chill."

"Yeah, whatever, Jamir, but I got a fucking son to feed, and I ain't got time to wait on a little something. How long you thought those bricks you gave me was gonna last? Huh? You ain't got the responsibilities I got, so you can chill for a minute. But me, nigga, I got to keep pushing on and provide for mine, so I'ma do it with or without you."

Jamir didn't want Danny to run up on Raw and Blount because it was his product they were moving. He wondered if he should warn them, just in case Danny really made a move, or if he should throw him one of the many bricks he had stashed away. He decided the latter option would be the best choice.

"Come on, D, you ain't got to be out here robbing these niggas, as long as you are part of my team. I got you something to get you back on your feet, but you got to invest the money you make from it this time. Until you do that, you gone stay behind."

"What you mean, invest this time? Break that shit down in hood terms."

"What I'm trying to tell you is that I'm going to give you a brick for nothing, but you got to take the money you make from it and invest it back into my product. You run that shit right, your bricks will begin to double, and then triple, and so on. You'll be a rich nigga in no time."

"Since when did you become and expert? And what you mean by investing back in your product? When the hell did you become the cake man?"

"Remember when I told you that I would one day be the king of the streets? Well, that day has finally come. I ain't fuck off with my money or my shit, so I got a few birds right now that are ready to fly. Now, I need to know that you ready too, and we good."

"You damn right I'm ready. I mean, I know I done had plenty dope to where I should be sitting lovely, but I give you word, this time I'm gone put my money back in the pot."

Jamir knew that Danny had only agreed so he could get the drugs. He never really expected Danny to do right, but he had to do something to keep him from running up on his people. The last thing his operation needed was a setback, and a jack move would definitely make one. Jamir assured Danny that he would be back in less than an hour with what he had promised him, but what he didn't expect was an interference that would make him run late.

It had been a while since his grandmother's number showed up on his phone. But for her to be calling him, he knew it had to be important, so he pressed the call button on his phone and listened.

"Jamir, honey, I don't know what has kept you away, but son, I need you to come over here right away."

"What's wrong, G-Ma? You a'ight? Missy a'ight?"

"Please, just come over. I don't want to tell you over the phone."

She hung up without another word and it caused Jamir to get a pain in his chest. He felt in his heart that whatever she was calling about had something to do with Missy. He hadn't heard anymore rumors of her buying dope, but she had been real scarce lately. She made it a habit of going to see him at least three times a week. But ever since the day she claimed to be going out of town with her friends, her routine had changed.

He pressed the gas and drove to his grandmother's house as quickly as he could, his heart beating faster with each minute that passed. When her house finally came to view, Jamir slowed down. He could feel his heart being torn from his chest before he even parked his car. When he got out of his car and walked up the steps that led to the front door, his hands began to shake. And as soon as his grandmother opened her door and looked into his eyes, he felt his heartbeat come to a standstill. No words needed to be said because Jamir already knew the signs.

Chapter 15

Missy's untimely death was felt all over the hood, and everyone on the block showed up to pay their respects. Jamir felt empty because he had lost the one person who meant more than anything to him. When he was told that she had died from an apparent overdose, he had the urge to kill A.J. all over again, even though he had never proved that she had bought dope from him. He couldn't understand what had led her down that path, especially after all they had gone through with their father, growing up. Jamir felt like her death was his karma, his payback for the set-up he did on Timbo. He knew that he would just have to swallow that shit no matter how hard it was.

Jamir watched with tear-filled eyes as the casket was lowered into the ground. He looked beside him and saw his grandmother as she wiped her weary eyes. He reached over and held her hand, a gesture he had not done since he was a little boy. The woman beside him had been there for him and his sister when no one else was, and he had disregarded her feelings for so long because of his own selfishness. He knew that she would never agree to what he was out doing in the streets. So to avoid a lecture, he just avoided her altogether. Jamir knew that he had been wrong, so he squeezed her small, wrinkled hand and apologized.

"I'm sorry for not going to see you since I moved out, but I'ma make it up to you."

"No, son, you owe me nothing. I know you've only been avoiding me because you didn't want me to scold you for what you are out there putting in the streets. But you are my only grandson and I only lecture you because I love you. Missy is gone. I don't want to lose you too, but you are gown, and it is not right for me to judge you. Just promise me that you will be careful. That's all I need from you."

Jamir pulled her into his arms and held her, while the dirt was thrown into the six-foot deep square that held the love of his life. He felt guilt for her passing because he did nothing to prevent it. He had been so busy doing his own thing that he neglected the one person that mattered the most in his life. He felt like he should have asked more questions, but he kept putting it off, waiting for signs that he would never see. He needed to know how and when she started her downward spiral and hoped that all those answers hadn't been buried with her. Jamir was determined to find out, but he knew it wouldn't be easy.

Once the funeral had ended and Jamir made sure his grandmother was okay, he decided that it was best for him to go home. He needed some time to himself to mourn the loss because it had been a huge one. There was a celebration of life get-together planned in Missy's memory, but as hard as Danny tried to get Jamir to stay for it, he just didn't have it in him. He couldn't fathom hanging out and eating a big plate of food, while his heart was in the ground, even though he knew the celebration was the norm.

Jamir looked around one last time at all who had come out, some he knew and others he had never seen before. He wondered why someone had to lose their life to bring unity to the hood, and realized it was just the way things were. He knew that the next day, all would be back to what it was before, as if nothing had ever happened. Missy would become only a memory to everyone but him. He would keep her alive through him, until he rested in peace beside her.

Jamir drove home, through the streets, slowly, and thought about his next move. He had to keep on pushing himself, no matter what. He knew that's what Missy would have wanted. Jamir pulled in his driveway and shut the engine off. But instead of getting out, he decided to sit there for a moment. He thought about the times Missy had come over, only for him to run her off, so he could handle his business. So many regrets filled his mind, but it was too late to make it all up.

"Rest in peace, baby sis. I give you my word that when I find out who got you on that shit, I'm sending them to hell."

Jamir finally got out and walked up the steps, so he could go inside to a place that would feel empty. He pushed his key into the lock, and as soon as he turned it, a voice he needed to hear came from behind him.

"Jamir, I'm sorry about your sister. I wanted to be there, but I didn't know how you would feel about it. But I'm here now. Please, just let me be here for you."

No sooner than he turned around to face Rachel, a tear slid from his eyes. The fact that she had shown up when he needed someone the most gave him a whole new respect for her. She was the last person he expected to see, but there she was in front of him, ready to take on his burden of sadness and loss. When she walked up closer to him and wrapped her arms around his waist, it was then that he let it all go. He felt no shame in his tears around her, and the comfort she brought him gave him a sense of peace. Maybe things really would be okay, hard, but still okay. All the reasons he had been upset with Rachel disappeared from his thoughts, as she took away the ache in his heart.

That night, Jamir held Rachel close to him, as if he never wanted to let her go. She hoped that it would open his eyes and make him realize that she was more than a crackhead. She was someone who had feelings and only wanted to be loved and understood. If only he would accept her as is, she could make him very happy.

The night came and went, without notice, and when Jamir opened his eyes and saw that she was still beside him, he smiled. He could feel his early morning hard on pressed against his boxers, so he reached down and set it free. No sooner than he did it, Rachel turned over and gripped his manhood with her hand. Slowly, she moved her hand up and down his shaft. She had missed that part of him, almost as much as she missed the rest of him. Without saying one word, she pulled the covers back, and as soon as her mouth embraced his hardness, he let out a low moan.

Jamir enjoyed the warmness of her mouth as he thought about what they could be together. He wondered if she really would leave the drugs alone, if he claimed her. But he wasn't sure that he was ready to face the embarrassment that came with it. He was well on his way to the top, but what would happen if he took her with him and she relapsed, only to bring him back down. What if she ended up like Missy? How would he be able to handle another tragic loss? He decided to make the best of the time he had right then, instead of worrying and wondering what could or could not be.

Jamir spent the rest of the day making love to the one person who made him feel something. Every time his cell phone rang, he sent it straight to voicemail. He wasn't about to let anyone disturb his groove, or at least, that's what he thought. The knock at his back door broke his concentration. He hoped that if he didn't answer, they would go away, but they were determined to get his attention. He got up and told Rachel to keep quiet while he went and answered the door. But as soon as he opened it, he regretted it because he didn't want to deal with who was behind it.

"I'm still pissed at you, Jamir, but I heard about your sister and wanted to come check on you. I figured that you might need a shoulder to lean so, so here I am."

"Um, yeah. Thanks, Erica, but I'm good. I just really don't want to be bothered right now. Maybe we can catch up another time."

Jamir started to close the door, but Erica walked inside before he could stop her. He found the move disrespectful, but he had to remember just who he was dealing with. He had to get her out of there though, before she realized who was in his bed. Jamir knew he should have been more careful, but he had been so lost in the moment with Rachel that he let the time slip away. He knew he should have made her leave the night before and now he had to face possible exposure to who he had been fucking with.

"Look, Erica, I'ma need you to leave. I got some shit I'm trying to handle right now, and you only gone be in my way. I'll hit you up later or something."

"Aw come on, Jamir. Let me chill with you for a little while. I know you're hurting inside and I'm sure I could think of a few things to make the heartache go away."

Erica walked up closer to him and tried to put her arms around him. As soon as he reached out to push her away, Rachel walked out of the bedroom, a move that would cause Jamir to become angry with her all over again.

"He said he wanted you to leave, so you should respect that and go."

When Erica turned to the female voice and saw who it was, she laughed. She couldn't even believe that Jamir had the nerve to have a druggie in his house, but she chalked it up to his recent loss. There was no way he had been thinking clearly and she wasn't about to let a crack smoker push her away.

"Damn, Jamir, you really are going through it, but you didn't have to stop and pick up a trick. You could have came to me. I wouldn't have turned you away, even after how you did me."

"I'm not here as a trick, so watch your mouth."

"Or what? Your crackhead ass ain't gonna do a damn thing. You only here to get his dick wet, and then he will send you on your way."

"That's funny because I've been here all night, and yet, you're the one he's telling to leave. Apparently, he wants me here. Don't you, Jamir?"

Jamir looked from Rachel to Erica but didn't answer the question. He knew that if he admitted to wanting Rachel there, it could hurt his reputation in the long run. But if he didn't, he could possibly lose her forever. He just couldn't make himself admit that she was more than a trick to him. He could see the pain fill her eyes as he stood there in silence. He couldn't believe he was being confronted in that way. He didn't owe Erica a damn thing, and yet, he still didn't want to reveal the truth.

"Ya know, I think that maybe both of you should leave. I need a little time to myself anyway."

"Yeah, trick, get the hell out. You probably done smoked up all of his shit anyway."

The words that came out of Erica's mouth stung Rachel's emotions. She stood silent and waited to see if Jamir would step up and defend her, but he said nothing. She couldn't believe that he would stand there and allow the next bitch to degrade her that way, when he knew it wasn't true. Something in her heart had told her to stay away, but the love she held for him made her keep going back. She decided that it would be the final time she would go to him, because she obviously meant nothing to him. Love wasn't supposed to hurt the way that it had, but it was like a sharp knife going straight through her heart.

When Rachel walked out of the room, Jamir held his head down because he knew he had fucked up. He should have said something in her defense, but he didn't want Erica to know that he gave a fuck about Rachel. Erica stood with her arms crossed over her chest as if she had won a contest, and it was only when Rachel walked out of Jamir's house that she spoke up.

"Well, hopefully you were able to keep some of your dope. Dumb bitch would have stayed here until you were completely dry."

"Erica, shut the fuck up and get the hell outta my house."

"Are you serious, Jamir? I just did your black ass a favor, and that's the appreciation I get for it?"

"No, you didn't do a damn thing for me because I wanted her here, and not as a trick. I don't have to give her drugs to make her want to be with me."

"So, you trying to make me believe that she was here in your bed as more than a trick? That's funny."

"Yeah, well I don't find shit funny about it. Rachel ain't the person you and everyone else thinks she is. And instead of taking up for her, I stood here and allowed you to treat her like shit. That's my bad, but that won't happen again. Now get the hell out and don't come here again."

"You know what? Fuck you, Jamir. I'ma tell the whole block that you feeling a bitch that all of them done ran through. You'll be the joke of the neighborhood, and ain't nobody gonna respect you after that. And you can keep the dick, ain't no telling who else that motherfucker done been in."

When Erica tried to walk past him, Jamir reached out and wrapped his hand around her throat. He pushed her back against the wall and stared into her eyes. The last thing he intended to do was be violent with a female, but once he lost Missy, the gender no longer mattered. Everyone would be at risk. He wanted to snap Erica's neck right then and there, but instead, he let her go. She began to cough and rubbed where his hand had been. She should have wanted to leave after that, but instead, she reached out and began to massage his dick, the very thing she never wanted again.

"Come on, Jamir, fuck me while you're angry. Show a bitch what happens when she defies you."

Jamir looked at Erica like she had lost her damn mind, but never once tried to remove her hand from his manhood.

What better way to put a bitch in their place and show them who ran shit? Jamir was about to be a boss, so he felt it was time to act like one. So when she pulled his dick out of the opening in his boxers, he didn't move. That ghetto ass shit had him turned the fuck on. He stood still while she deep throated his length. He knew that he was wrong to allow her to continue, but the way she had his toes curling had him gone. When she finally made him nut, she swallowed his seed and then began to suck him back to life.

"Stand up and take that shit off so a nigga can feel you."

She thought he would never ask. She allowed his dick to fall from her mouth and smiled. Erica knew that she had him right where she wanted him. All men were suckers for some good head, and she knew that she had the best in town. At least, that's what all the niggas who'd had it had told her. She didn't think that Jamir knew how much she got around. If he did, he might deem her no better than the white girl. She felt like if she could trap him and make him her nigga, she would be set.

Once Erica took off all her clothes, she sat in the only chair in the area and began to touch herself. She didn't have to do it for very long because Jamir had rocked up immediately. He loved that freaky shit, so much that he forgot to put on a condom before he made Erica bend over. He entered her from behind and put in that work.

"That's right, Jamir, show a bitch what you working with. You a boss ass nigga, and this pussy is all yours."

***

Rachel had only made it a couple of blocks when she realized she had forgotten her bag at Jamir's house. She really didn't want to walk back for it, but she had no other choice. That bag held everything she needed. The thought of facing him again made her sick on her stomach, but what else could she do? She just hoped that Erica had left by then because she didn't want to hear another word from her.

She still couldn't believe that the bitch said all those awful things to her, and Jamir just stood there and let her. She wondered if he knew of all her indiscretions because she wasn't completely innocent. Erica had tricked with plenty of niggas, some of them for drugs. She just did a better job at hiding her habit, so very few people knew about it. Rachel wanted to put her on blast, but she had never been the messy type and wasn't about to let a nobody like Erica change that. Jamir would just have to find out the hard way, hopefully, before it was too late.

When Jamir's house came into view, Rachel let out a sigh of relief. She felt like it had taken forever to walk the distance back. Thankfully, his car still sat in the driveway. She felt nervous having to face him again and hoped she didn't fall weak.

Rachel was just about to knock on his back door when she heard the sounds of sex coming from the other side. She thought that she was imagining things, so she put her ear to the door, and sure enough, a bitch was moaning and calling Jamir's name. When she realized the bitch sounded like Erica, she reached out and put her hand on the doorknob. Rachel turned it slowly and found that it was unlocked. She pushed it open carefully because she wanted to see things for herself. When she was sure that it was indeed Erica, she opened the door the rest of the way.

Jamir was deep in the pussy, when he felt a light breeze on his back. He was focused on the matter at hand and didn't want to stop, but the chill was bothering him. He pulled out of Erica so he could see where it was coming from. When he turned around and looked into Rachel's eyes, the breeze no longer mattered.

"I'm sorry, but I forgot my bag."

Rachel walked past him and went into his room. Once she got her bag, she walked back out and slammed the door behind her. Jamir knew he had really fucked up and felt his heart shatter all over again.

Chapter 16

For the next several months, Jamir put all his energy into the streets. His grandmother had grown ill and died peacefully in her sleep, but he knew that her cause of death was a broken heart. He had no one but himself, and that's exactly who he focused on. The bitterness inside of him ate him up, and he became a different man.

Danny sat beside him and rolled up some kush as Jamir carefully watched him. He wanted to make sure the blunt wasn't laced because he felt like getting his buzz on. Once it was rolled, Danny lit it and passed it to a waiting Jamir.

"Here ya go, bruh. Shit right here is going to have you on your ass real quick."

"See, that's where ya wrong. Can't nothing put a nigga like me on they ass. I'm too mufuckin' thorough for that."

Jamir put the blunt to his lips and pulled really hard. He had to admit, the shit was that chronic, and he felt it instantly. He took another pull and passed it back to Danny. He needed to stay on point because he was on a mission. Jamir focused his eyes back up the street. He had been waiting on A.J. to hit the block because he was about to give his ass that heat. He felt like he had let the shit go long enough.

Missy's death still ate him up inside, and he would not rest until he took care of everyone who had a hand in it. Jamir needed to send a message out to the block, so no one else ever tried him. He felt like if he would have acted sooner, Missy would still be alive and wrecking his nerves.

"There go that nigga right there." Danny pointed down the block.

When Jamir saw that he had pointed out A.J., Jamir nodded his head and pulled out his gun. He had told Malcolm that he was going to let it go, but it made him feel like a pussy. He would give A.J. two options to choose from. He could either get off his block or get knocked off his block. Either way, Jamir never wanted to see his face again. Jamir tapped Danny, letting him know that it was time to make a move. Both got out of the car and walked into the darkness to where A.J. was posted up. Before he knew they were there, they had their guns pointed at his chest.

"Whoa, Jamir, the fuck is you doing?"

"Nigga, you don't think I know about you selling my sister that shit? Huh? You knew better than to disrespect me like that, but you ain't give a damn. Mufucka, my baby sister is gone, and now you got to suffer."

"Hold up. I only sold it to her that one time, but she told me it was for her friend, not her. A nigga would never do you like that. You gotta believe me."

"It ain't matter who she was getting it for, you knew it was a violation of the streets."

"Come on, Jamir. Now you know if she wouldn't have got it from me, she would have gotten it from someone else, and ain't no telling what they would have gave her."

Jamir hit A.J. upside the head with the butt of his gun and brought him to his knees, while Danny stood to the side and watched the exchange. He had never thought Jamir had it in him to be a killer, so he couldn't wait to see how things turned out. Danny was thankful that he had never found out about him turning Missy out on the drugs, because that could have very well been him on his knees.

"I'ma give you two choices, and how this turns out depends on which one you choose. Now, you can either pack up your shit and get off this block, or you can eat one of these bullets."

"How you gonna try to get me off the block, when I been out here longer than you? Missy gone, Jamir, and no matter what you do or how many mufuckas you kill, she ain't coming back. Let that shit go, bruh. It ain't my fault she's dead."

Another hit on the dome knocked A.J. on his ass. Of all the times he had his boys out there with him, he had told them to take the night off. He never knew that he had a death warrant, until then, but he would not go out like a chump. He had served on that very same block for years and wouldn't give up his spot that easy. Jamir would just have to take it. A.J. knew that he was going to die, so he antagonized Jamir in hopes to get it over with.

"Ya daddy ain't never teach you that if you point a gun, you better use it?"

"Nigga, I ain't got no daddy."

"Oh, you got one. He just lost on that pipe. Don't be mad at me because Missy followed in his footsteps."

"You mufucka, don't ever say her name out of your dick sucker again."

Danny wondered what was taking Jamir so long to pull the trigger. He had grown tired of standing there and listening to him and A.J. go back and forth. He had asked Jamir to let him be the trigger man, but he told him that it was his responsibility to do it. Danny could tell that Jamir was doing everything possible to avoid a murder that needed to happen. So, Danny edged him on.

"Come on, Mir. The fuck is you waiting on? That nigga should have been leaking as soon as he told you he wasn't going anywhere. Now do it and let's go."

Jamir took one look at Danny and then turned his focus back on A.J. He knew that if he didn't pull the trigger, it would come back to haunt him, and he would end up being the victim. Jamir wasn't ready to die because he wanted to live long enough to leave behind a legacy, so A.J. would have to go. Danny had asked him if he wanted him to pull the

154

trigger, but Jamir needed to handle the job, mainly to make him feel less guilt about not protecting Missy like he should have.

Jamir took one glance up to the sky and then pulled the trigger. Blood and brain matter hit him the face, but it didn't seem to bother him. He felt a sudden rush of adrenaline and smiled. He never knew that taking a life could feel so good. He wished that he had done it sooner.

Jamir stood over A.J.'s dead body in a daze, until he felt Danny tap him on the shoulder.

"Come on, Mir. We got to get the hell outta here before someone sees us. Nigga, I ain't trying to go to jail."

Thankfully, Jamir listened, and the two of them ran back to his ride and drove off. The next day, the talk of the block was all about A.J.'s murder. No one even knew he had enemies, but they understood that it came with being a street dealer. A.J.'s baby momma came out and identified his body because his own momma didn't want to see him like that. She wanted to remember him as he was. After a few days, things went back to normal around the block.

Jamir and Danny were sitting outside of old man Nate's when Jamir brought up an idea.

"So, D, how you feel about recruiting mufuckas to join the team? Give us a chance to expand out."

"Why we need to recruit? I think we doing very well out here on our own. Too many hands in the pot brings heat. I don't know about you, but I ain't trying to get burned."

"I agree, but we could cover more area if we had more bodies. I'm trying to build an empire and more income will help me reach that goal even faster."

"So who you got your eyes on? If you suggesting it, you already know who you want."

"I was thinking about Raw and her partner, Blount."

"Hell no, you know that bitch is my opp."

"Come on, D, that shit happened a long time ago. Don't you think you should move on? You shame 'cause a bitch left you for a bitch?"

"Fuck you, Jamir. I can assure you it wasn't because I ain't throw this dick right. Bitch just wanted her pussy ate, and I ain't sticking my mouth anywhere another man's dick has been."

"Never say never, nigga. Don't knock that shit till you try it."

"What? You men to tell me you done ate some pussy? I thought only white boys did that, but now I know not to pull on a spliff behind your ass."

"Whatever, but you don't know what you're missing. Anyway, I'ma push on past that subject and get back to what we was talking about. How you feel about pulling Raw and her people in?"

"Ya know, Jamir, you my boy and I ain't never known you to make dumb moves. Because of that, I'll call a truce with Raw, but don't let her around any of my bitches."

And that was how Jamir began his crew. Danny would never find out that Raw had been working for Jamir for a while, and that was how they kept it. Raw even pulled her cousin, Smack, from New York, and together they, Jamir and his crew, made the streets bleed cocaine and crack. Jamir could afford to finally sit back and enjoy what he had built. His cocaine habit had also grown with his bank account. He snorted the drug as soon as he woke up in the morning and all throughout the day. He also no longer hid it from Danny.

"Damn, nigga, you full time on that blow. Don't you think you should slow down?"

"Don't worry, D, a nigga still has control. I'm still running shit ain't I?"

"Yeah, you are, but I remember the days when you would tell me the same thing. I just don't want you to get beside yourself and slip up."

"I'm good, but thanks for looking out."

Money had been coming in from all directions and was building up quickly. Jamir still had his connection with the Colombians and with Malcolm, so the flow of cocaine never ran out. Jamir thought that he had built a good team of soldiers. They proved to be loyal and trustworthy, so Jamir began to relax his hand. It felt good to be able to sit back and let the money come to him. But he knew that when shit started going good, something bad was bound to happen.

"Jamir, I'm pregnant."

"So what the hell you telling me for?"

"Really, Jamir, now you know I ain't been with nobody but you, so you might as well accept the fact that you gone be a daddy."

"I ain't claiming shit until we get a DNA test, so you can go somewhere with that."

"What you mean, go somewhere? Nigga, I need money for doctor's appointments and baby supplies."

"Then I suggest you get a job because I ain't giving you shit, until I know for a fact that baby is mine. You ain't gone trap me like that."

"Ain't nobody trying to trap your ass. Just know that I will be back."

Jamir couldn't believe that he had fucked around and got Erica pregnant. He knew the baby could possibly be his because he had been running up in her raw for a minute. He couldn't believe that he had slipped up like that. He knew his grandmother was probably rolling over in her grave because she had raised him better than that. When he told Danny, he was shocked because Jamir always claimed that he wasn't going to plant seeds, and that was exactly what he had done.

"So what you gone do now? Nigga, you at the top of your game. The last thing you need is a fucking baby. Trust me, I know from experience."

"I don't know, D. I just got caught up in the moment. Shit was a mistake and now, my black ass is fucked."

"You damn right you are. You gone feel my pain because having a baby mama, especially at our age, is a fucking headache. Now you can see how easy it was for me to despise Trish."

When it came time for Erica to have the baby, Jamir was right there, not because he really wanted to be, but because he felt obligated. When the DNA test came back as him being the father, he knew he had to step up. Jamir refused to be a deadbeat dad like his was, so he went out and got everything Erica and his baby daughter needed. She had tried to talk him into letting them live with him, but he told her no. Jamir refused to have his space invaded, so he put her up in her own apartment. He told Erica that he would make sure they were taken care of, but he didn't want to fuck with her like that anymore. She seemed to understand and took it better than he thought.

Jamir had left the small apartment he had put Erica up in and was on his way home, when he saw Rachel standing in front of old man Nate's. She had been gone for close to a year, and he thought he would never see her again. He couldn't lie, he still felt deep for her in his heart. There was no way he could just drive by and not say something, so he pulled over and rolled his window down.

"Sup, Rachel? When did you get back in town?"

"Oh, hey, Jamir. You sure you want to be seen talking to me out here?"

"Look, I'm sorry for not stepping in and saying something when Erica treated you like that. Let me make it up to you."

"And why would you want to do that? You have moved on with your life. So please, let me move on with mine, too."

"Come on, ma, I apologized. Don't that count for something?"

"Your apologies don't mean a damn thing to me anymore, Jamir. You knew how I felt about you and yet, you continued to step on my feelings. You let that bitch talk to me like I wasn't shit, and then you turned right around and fucked her after I left. You cared so much about your reputation, and all I needed was for you to care about me. I won't allow you to pull me back in, Jamir. Loving you hurts too bad, and I'm just not going to do it anymore."

"So you can just stop loving me like that?"

"I've moved on and found someone who ain't ashamed to call me his, but you will always hold a place in my heart."

About that time, Jason Barnes walked out of Nate's and put his arm around Rachel. Jason was a rival dealer from the other side of town. He had gone big time a couple of years earlier, but he only dealt in cocaine and heroin. Jason only dealt with niggas who were spending ten grand and up, so crack was not on his menu. Jamir wondered how Rachel had hooked him, and it bothered him to know that she was moving on without him. Jamir felt bad for how he had done her. Having a daughter gave him a whole new outlook on a lot of things. He couldn't imagine his daughter growing up and being treated any type of way by a man, even if she was flawed.

Jamir stayed up that night and thought about Rachel. He couldn't believe he had let her slip away, and he lay there trying to think of ways to get her back. He knew that it would cause Erica and him to fall out, but he didn't give a fuck, as long as he could still see his daughter. He woke up the next day and called Danny to meet him. He had come up with a plan and was ready to pull it off.

"We gone run up on Barnes and take everything he's got."

"You mean Jason Barnes? What that nigga do to you?"

"He's got something that belongs to me. You down or what? I mean, I could go get Raw to help me pull it off."

"Now you already know that you can depend on me. When you want to do it?"

"As soon as possible."

***

Jamir thought shit would be good, since Danny agreed to help him do the jack, but what he didn't know was that Jason had seen it in his eyes and was already up on game. He questioned Rachel and she told him how she felt about Jamir, and the reason why they weren't together. He could only respect her honesty. He decided to step to Jamir like a man and let him know that whatever he had planned wasn't necessary.

Jamir was sitting outside on his front porch, nursing a blunt, when Jason pulled up. Jamir stood and rested his hand on his weapon because he wasn't sure of what else to do. He kept his eyes on Jason as he got out of his ride and walked up to him.

"You can relax, Jamir. You ain't gone need that weapon. I'm only here on a peace talk."

"The fuck is you talking about?"

"You know exactly what I'm talking about. I saw that shit in your eyes that day outside of Nate's. I want you to think about it before you make a move. You doing pretty good for yourself, and making a move on me ain't going to get you anywhere, especially with Rachel."

"I don't know what you implying, brotha, so why don't you break that shit down so I can understand?"

"I know you planning to come in and pull a jack move. I know the look. Ain't no sense in starting a war because of one woman, when we can work that shit out amongst ourselves. You already on the rise, and from what I see, you only going to go higher. Let's call a truce right here, right now. I'll let her go, but you have to let go of those thoughts you have about moving in on me. I suggest that if she means so much to you, show her, because the next man might not be so generous."

With that said, Jason stood and held his hand out. Jamir hesitated but ultimately reached out and shook his hand. They had made a deal, and Jamir would keep his end of the bargain. Jason had been right. A war was not needed, but going after him would have brought one. He wondered if Danny had said something, or if Jason really did just see it coming. He had started to put a little trust in his boy and would be really disappointed if he found out Danny went behind his back. There was only one way to find out.

"Aye, D, you ain't talked to that nigga we planned that move on, have you?"

"Why the hell would I talk to him? And speaking of that move, I'm ready when you are."

"I've been thinking about that, and I decided to call it off."

"What you mean, nigga? I had my gat loaded and ready to go. You turning pussy on me now?"

"Nah, I just think it's a bad move. I'm at the top of my game, and it's only going to cause me a setback, something I don't need right now."

"Hold up a minute. I thought you said he had something that belonged to you?"

"He did, but he agreed to return it, so I'ma let that nigga keep breathing."

"What you mean? Didn't you ask me if I had talked to that nigga? Now you telling me you and him made an agreement about returning something to you? What kind of game you playing here, Jamir?"

"Look, that nigga showed up at my house. And I ain't gone lie to you, I thought you had put him up on game. But he claimed that he could see it in my eyes. I just wanted to make sure he was telling the truth."

"So you thought I done went behind your back and betrayed you? What type of nigga do you think I am? I've always had your back on everything, Jamir. I thought you knew that."

"I do, and I was just tripping because I ain't tell nobody else about it. I just found that shit crazy that he knew."

"Yeah, you was tripping, but I'ma let that shit slide because you my boy. Just don't think like that again."

Jamir felt bad about feeling like Danny had sold him out. Ever since he tried to up the money Timbo had asked for, Jamir had seen a change in him. He could tell that Danny was trying to be a better person. He had let the shit go with Raw, and he had been spending more time with Trish. He was glad that he was finally on the right track.

The two of them decided to let the shit go and pick up the rest of the crew for a night at the strip club. It was packed and the bitches were thick in all the right places. Jamir got him and his crew a table in the VIP area because he wanted to be where he could see everything. When the waitress went over to take their drink order, Danny tried to put his mack down, but she was more interested in Raw. When Danny realized it, he just held his hands up and turned to focus elsewhere.

Jamir got his first lap dance from a big booty red bone. Her ass completely swallowed the thongs that she had on, but for some reason, it didn't turn him on. He went ahead and let her finish her set before giving her a stack of bills. She tried to stick around, but Jamir sent her on her way. The entire crew blew at least a grand a piece and had a good time. It had been a nice break from the block, but they all knew it would be back to business the next day.

They finally left the club around one a.m. When Jamir dropped all of them off, he headed straight home. He had no reason to stay out on the block because the fiends seemed to all be inside. It was too late for him to go by and check on his daughter. He knew she would be asleep, and he didn't feel like being bothered with Erica, anyway. He was just about to turn down his street when he saw Rachel. He pulled up beside her and hit the locks on his doors. She hesitated at first, but then opened the door and got in. She had so much she wanted to say to him, but found herself unable to say anything at all.

He drove the rest of the way without one word. When he pulled in his driveway, they both got out and walked up his front steps. Jamir opened his front door and moved so she could walk in first, and then he walked in behind her. He made sure to lock his door so there wouldn't be any surprises, and then the two of them went to his bedroom. Jamir laid down and made room for her to lay beside him. He wondered what Jason had said to her to make her leave, or if she chose to do it on her own. He didn't want to question her and ruin the moment, so he just held her instead. He knew that he didn't deserve her, but he didn't think anyone else did either. Just as he was about to close his eyes, she finally spoke.

"Jason told me what you had planned to do, but I don't understand why, and I don't understand you."

"It was a bad call, but it was the only thing I could think of to do."

"He knew how I felt about you, Jamir, and he knew that as long as you were breathing, I'd always come back to you. I was fine until I saw you. I thought I would be strong enough to leave you alone, but my love won't let me."

"You don't have to worry, Rachel, and I know you're going to anyway, but I'm ready to have you in my life. I want to move away from here, and I want you with me. My money seems right, and I done pulled some power moves, so we can get up out of this hood. Just me and you, but only if you want to."

"I'll go anywhere with you, but don't think that what you already have ain't good enough, because it is."

"I know, and that's why you mean so much to me, but a nigga has cul-de-sac dreams baby. I ain't about to live like this forever."

"Jamir, have you ever dreamed of being anything else?"

"Hell nah. I knew I was destined to be a dope boy from the time I stopped shitting in diapers. Besides, I don't qualify for anything else. A nigga got skills in the streets and here in the bed with you. Why? You don't like my career?"

"I'm just saying, there are safer things to do."

"Yeah, Rachel, there are, but those jobs are for white boys. Niggas like me get looked over. Selling dope and stacking paper is what's expected of a black man. That, or going out and robbing mufuckas. The crackas don't feel like we good enough to do anything else, so I stay in my lane and stay the fuck out of theirs. Besides, I got a daughter to take care of now, and that legal money don't come fast enough."

Rachel was confused by what he'd said. She had been away for a minute, so she hadn't heard anything about Jamir having a daughter. It broke her heart to think that another woman had a piece of him. She had hoped to be the one who gave him that gift, but her hopes had been shattered. She couldn't understand why shit in her world had to be so complicated. Jamir noticed her sudden silence and wondered what was wrong.

"What's up? Why you went quiet on me?"

"I didn't know, Jamir. When did you have a daughter?"

"Come on, now. Shit just happened, and I fucked up, but don't let that spoil what we got going on. It don't change anything between us."

Jamir pulled her closer, but it didn't ease her mind. Rachel wanted all of him, but now, she would have to settle for a piece. She wasn't sure if she could do that. As she lay in his arms, she thought about her options. She had fought for so long for his love and affection, and now that she had it out in the open, she didn't know if she wanted it anymore. Rachel had finally got off drugs and wanted to live a drama free life, but with a baby momma on the side, that would never happen.

"Jamir, who's the mother of your daughter?"

He didn't want to answer the question, but what else could he do? Rachel would find out anyway. How could he tell her that the one who he allowed to treat her like shit was the one who held a piece of his heart? He knew he should have kept his dick in his pants, but it was too late, so he told Rachel what she wanted to know. He would just have to deal with the consequences later.

Chapter 17

"I knew you had a thing for that crackhead, and now you're telling me you want to be out in the open with her. Nigga, you is crazy. How you think Erica is going to take that news?"

"Fuck Erica, she ain't my bitch, and Rachel ain't a crackhead no more. She done cleaned that shit up. Besides, the only reason Erica is still in my life is because of my daughter, but she doesn't run a damn thing."

"A'ight, Mir, but I can't wait to see how that shit plays out."

Jamir and Danny were on their way to meet up with Raw. Shit had begun to get heavy in the streets, and they needed to discuss their strategy plan before the drama came their way. Police presence had made it harder to be out on the streets. There had been a high number of robberies and bodies had been falling. Business was slow, but Jamir and his crew knew the show must go on. They couldn't afford to hide out like a bunch of pussies. They would just have to be on high alert, especially because no one seemed to know who was pulling off the jack moves.

Jamir understood that having enemies was all part of the game. He just didn't know that the enemies were his own, but he would soon find out. When he pulled up in Raw's front yard, he found it kind of strange that she was already waiting on him. The scene felt all wrong and caused Jamir to put a hand on his weapon. He saw Danny make the same move but instead of just putting a hand on it, he pulled it out from his waist and pointed it at Jamir.

"You can go ahead and hand me that because you won't be needing it."

"The hell you doing, D?"

"Just do what I said, and then get out slowly. Don't try no slick shit, Mir. I don't want to have to pull this trigger too soon."

Jamir shook his head and passed his gun to Danny. He couldn't believe his luck. It seemed like every time he was almost at the top, something happened to push him back down. He wasn't sure what was going to happen that day, but he was determined to walk away with his life. He had worked too hard to get to where he was to give up that easily. He had known for a while that he couldn't trust Danny, but he never suspected Raw to be down to betray him. He took one last look at Danny before Raw opened his door with a gun pointed at his head.

"You know what it is, nigga. Get your ass on out so we can get this over with."

"A'ight, I'm getting out, but somebody got to tell me what the fuck is going on."

"Ain't nobody got to tell you a damn thing. In case you haven't noticed, you don't run shit anymore. Those days are over, bruh. There's a new boss in town, now move."

Jamir stepped out of his ride and shut the door behind him. He regretted it a soon as he did because if he had a chance to get away, the door being left open would have made it much easier. He knew it was too late to make the move, so he just stood there and looked at Danny. Jamir wondered when Danny and Raw had become partners because last he checked, they still couldn't stand each other. He thought they worked together on the business tip because of him, but the truth had finally come out.

"Go ahead and make your way inside, and don't try nothing stupid because we will be on your ass."

Jamir wondered if Blount was inside the house waiting on him, but he got his answer as soon as he walked in. The house was eerily quiet and not a soul was in sight. He noticed that Tomeka wasn't even there. Jamir was on his own and all he could do was hope that he made it out of there alive. He wasn't sure exactly where he was supposed to go, but he could feel the tip of Raw's gun poking him in the back.

"You know where to go, nigga. The meeting place is still the same."

Jamir walked into the kitchen with Danny and Raw close behind. He thought about his daughter and wished that he had spent more time with her. She was still just a baby and too young to understand the street side of shit. He hoped that Erica would make sure his memory stayed fresh in his little girl's mind. He then thought of Rachel and wondered if she would go back to getting high without him in her life. When Missy and his grandmother came to mind, a tear fell from his eye. They were both angels in Heaven, but he felt like he would go to hell and would never be able to make things right with them. Jamir had lived a good life, but still, there were so many regrets. His heart ached at the betrayal of his crew, but there was nothing he could do about it. Raw's voice broke him from his thoughts and emotions.

"Now see, we can do this the easy way or the hard way. It's your choice."

"The fuck you niggas want from me? I done opened up a world of opportunity for y'all, and this is what I get in return?" Jamir then turned his focus on Danny. "Come on, D, we done been through the mud and you turning on me for her?"

"Yeah, Mir, you close to being right. We have been through the mud, but how many times did you walk around it and left me stuck in the middle of it? You always talked about we equals, but every time I read the scales, that shit was off balance."

"Nah, D, if it was off balance, it was because you made it that way. I had my shit together and you was always careless, but can you tell me this? Was you fucking with Missy behind my back?"

"Hell no. She was like a sister to me, and you know that. Why don't you just let her rest in peace?"

The lie had been so easy for Danny to tell because he had told it for so long. He felt bad for the way he had got Missy hooked on drugs and knew that it was partly his fault that she was gone. He hoped that Jamir would never find out, and so far he hadn't. Danny felt like he had been put on the spot with the question about Missy, so he looked at Raw to take things back over.

"A'ight, that's enough with the questions. It's your turn to answer some now. How you answer will determine your fate. We need to know where the stash is at, and of course, the money."

"Fuck you, bitch. You gone kill me regardless, so I ain't telling shit."

"Now come on, Jamir, you know I'm a woman of my word. I'ma let you live, you just gone have a little bit of a different lifestyle."

"The fuck you mean by that?"

Raw picked up a syringe that she had lying on the table. She held it up, tapped the side of it, and then pushed the stick to release some of the contents it held. She looked at Danny, who only nodded his head, and then looked back at Jamir.

"This right here is that top quality heroin. Be having those mufuckin' junkies losing they minds. I'm telling you, Jamir, this shit is what's happening. You gone love it."

"So you think I'ma let you push that shit in me without a fight? Mufucka, you might as well go 'head and put a hot one in my dome, 'cause what you got planned ain't happening."

"Shit, nigga, Missy ain't complain."

169

Jamir jumped up as soon as Raw mentioned his sister's name. He wondered if it was her that administered the fatal dose that caused Missy's death. How could he have been so blind by the streets that he didn't see what was happening in his own backyard? Shit just didn't make any sense. With two guns pointed at him, Jamir decided to sit back down until he could figure a way out of what was happening.

"You killed my fucking sister? Why? Missy hadn't ever done shit to anybody. She was innocent in all this. She had a whole life ahead of her. Why didn't you come at me and spare her?"

"Well, I figured taking her would cause you more pain. And I ain't gone lie, I just wanted to see you suffer. Your ass been on a high rise ever since your paper went up, and I just needed you to see that you ain't never getting to the top."

"And you think you and Danny gone hold that spot? I thought you mufuckas still had some beef over pussy. When did that change?"

"It changed when you pushed so hard for us to call a truce. We did just what you asked us to do, so now it's time you do what we ask. So, once again, where is the stash and money?"

"Bitch, suck my dick."

Suddenly, Raw hit Jamir in the head with the butt of her gun and caused a gash. The blood dripped down on to his t-shirt, and he could feel the wetness of it seep through. He looked over at Danny, who sat there emotionless, and wished that he could somehow get through to him. Jamir's head ached from the sudden blow, but the pain didn't outweigh his desire to live. He knew that he needed to stall things for as long as he could. When Raw sat back down, he laughed at her because, honestly, the shit she had pulled had to be a joke.

"You find something funny because you seem to be the only mufucka laughing?"

"Yeah, I find this shit real funny. You doing all this extra shit to try to get to where I been at, while D ass sitting back letting you do all the work. But what neither of you realize is that y'all ain't wise enough to hold down my spot. A nigga like me been working all my life for this. Being a boss takes skills that neither of you mufuckas are equipped with. Don't matter to me what you do, but you wasting your time because I ain't giving up shit."

Danny finally stood and waked around the table to where Jamir was sitting. He towered over him and looked down. The two of them had been partners for a long time. They had gone from drinking out of dirty cups to sitting fine china on coasters, but Jamir had always been a step ahead.

Danny paced back and forth, without one word, as Jamir and Raw waited to see what he was about to do. The silence in the room was awkward and uncomfortable. Jamir looked from Raw to Danny and felt like he could possibly make a run for it, but just as soon as the thought entered his mind, it went away. He was a man, and he'd be damned if he died a coward. He knew this moment would come sooner or later, and decided to use his own tactics to turn the shit around.

"Ya know what, fuck you mufuckas, you can have all the shit because a nigga like me is destined to rise, and I'ma always get back up. That shit don't mean a damn thing to me."

Danny stopped pacing when Jamir spoke up. He knew Jamir very well and refused to believe that he would give up what he had worked for that easily, but Raw was naive.

"Now see how easy it is just to cooperate and get the shit over with?"

"Yeah, but I'ma have to take you to where it's at because you'll never find it on your own."

"Try me. I'm pretty good at following directions."

"Well what happened to you following the directions of the streets? What happened to your fucking loyalty? Or have you ever had any?"

"My loyalty is to me and who the hell I choose to give it to, and you are not included in that. I been out on them corners a long time but mufuckas look down on me because I'm a female. They don't think I got what it takes to be the man on top, but I'm 'bout to show them streets what I'm made of, just as soon as you give me what I asked for. Hell, you ain't gone need it because you gone be somewhere in a trap house with a needle in your arm, nodding off. But don't worry nigga, I'll let you suck my partner's dick to get you a fix."

Jamir was so angry inside, he jumped up out of the chair he sat in and punched Raw in the jaw. He swore that he could hear her bones crack, but at that moment, he didn't give a damn. He kept on swinging. He was going to beat her ass until he couldn't fight anymore. Jamir was waiting for the moment when Danny would defend her and pull the trigger, but he just stood on the side and watched. Suddenly, Raw found some strength and was able to push Jamir off of her, and before he had a chance to get up, she had the syringe stuck in his arm.

Everything became cloudy and the room felt like it was spinning. Jamir could hear Raw's voice, but couldn't make out what she was saying. All of a sudden, it felt like he was floating in the air, but he soon realized that he was being picked up. Raw and Danny sat him upright in the chair he had sat in before, and then slowly he put their words together.

"Damn, Danny, why the hell you let that nigga beat my ass like that?"

"Shit, you wanna be a mufuckin' man so bad, you should be able to fight like one."

"What the fuck ever, man. Let's tie his ass up so we can get what we need out of him. I was gone spare his ass, but that mufucka got to die today."

Jamir found it strange that his senses slowly came back, but he played it off. He watched Danny sit back down across from him, while Raw pulled up her chair in front of him to begin her reign of questioning again.

"Now, we gone try this one more time before I bust a cap in your ass. You should have just gave me the info I wanted, and it wouldn't have come to this. Now, where in the fuck is the stash?"

Jamir had begun to get drowsy all over again, but he managed to find the strength to spit in Raw's face. That seemed to piss her off even more. She'd had enough of Jamir's bullshit and decided that she would figure out where the stash was on her own. Time was of the essence, and she couldn't afford to keep sitting there wasting it. She pulled her gun back out and pointed it at Jamir's head, but changed her mind about pulling the trigger.

"Ya know, Danny, I think I'ma let you have the pleasure of killing this bastard. You been his underling long enough. Show this mufucka who the real boss is."

Danny stood from the chair he had been sitting in. Shit had finally come to a head, and it was time to leave his mark and show the streets what he was about. He pulled out his weapon again and walked around the table. Jamir sat tied up in the chair with his head bobbling up and down, in and out of consciousness.

Danny looked up at Raw and smiled before he cocked his gun and sent a bullet to the chamber. Raw was confused because she thought he had been ready to shoot the whole time. It didn't matter, though, as long as he was ready then. Danny then put the tip of his gun to the back of Jamir's dome. He had waited for this day to come for so long, and it was finally time to do what he should have done a long time ago.

"Go 'head, mufucka. What you waiting on? Pull the trigger."

Danny positioned his finger on the trigger and did exactly what he was told to do.

To be continued...

173

COMING SOON

Corner Boy Chronicles 2: Bury Me A Boss

Like me on Facebook
@AuthorCoreyRobinson

Lock Down Publications and Ca$h Presents
Assisted Publishing Packages

BASIC PACKAGE	UPGRADED PACKAGE
$499	$800
Editing	Typing
Cover Design	Editing
Formatting	Cover Design
	Formatting
ADVANCE PACKAGE	**LDP SUPREME PACKAGE**
$1,200	$1,500
Typing	Typing
Editing	Editing
Cover Design	Cover Design
Formatting	Formatting
Copyright registration	Copyright registration
Proofreading	Proofreading
Upload book to Amazon	Set up Amazon account
	Upload book to Amazon
	Advertise on LDP, Amazon and Facebook Page

***Other services available upon request.
Additional charges may apply

Lock Down Publications
P.O. Box 944
Stockbridge, GA 30281-9998
Phone: 470 303-9761

Submission Guideline

Submit the first three chapters of your completed manuscript to ldpsubmissions@gmail.com. In the subject line add **Your Book's Title**. The manuscript must be in a Word Doc file and sent as an attachment. Document should be in Times New Roman, double spaced, and in size 12 font. Also, provide your synopsis and full contact information. If sending multiple submissions, they must each be in a separate email.

Have a story but no way to send it electronically? You can still submit to LDP/Ca$h Presents. Send in the first three chapters, written or typed, of your completed manuscript to:

LDP: Submissions Dept
P.O. Box 944
Stockbridge, GA 30281-9998

DO NOT send original manuscript. Must be a duplicate. Provide your synopsis and a cover letter containing your full contact information.

Thanks for considering LDP and Ca$h Presents.

NEW RELEASES

BLOODLINE OF A SAVAGE 1&2
THESE VICIOUS STREETS
RELENTLESS GOON
RELENTLESS GOON 2
BY PRINCE A. TAUHID

THE BUTTERFLY MAFIA 1-3
BY FUMIYA PAYNE

A THUG'S STREET PRINCESS 1&2
BY MEESHA

CITY OF SMOKE 2
BY MOLOTTI

STEPPERS 1,2&3
BY KING RIO

THE LANE 1&2
BY KEN-KEN SPENCE

THUG OF SPADES 1&2
LOVE IN THE TRENCHES 2
BY COREY ROBINSON

TIL DEATH 3
BY ARYANNA

THE BIRTH OF A GANGSTER 4
BY DELMONT PLAYER

CORNER BOY | COREY ROBINSON

PRODUCT OF THE STREETS 1&2
BY DEMOND "MONEY" ANDERSON

NO TIME FOR ERROR
BY KEESE

MONEY HUNGRY DEMONS
BY TRANAY ADAMS

Coming Soon from Lock Down Publications/Ca$h Presents

IF YOU CROSS ME ONCE 6
ANGEL V
By Anthony Fields

IMMA DIE BOUT MINE 4&5
By Aryanna

A THUGS STREET PRINCESS 3
By Meesha

PRODUCT OF THE STREETS 3
By Demond Money Anderson

CORNER BOYS
By Corey Robinson

SON OF A DOPE FIEND 4
By Renta

THE MURDER QUEENS 6&7
By Michael Gallon

CITY OF SMOKE 3
By Molotti

BETRAYAL OF A G
By Ray Vinci

CONFESSIONS OF A DOPE BOY
By Nicholas Lock

THA TAKEOVER
By Keith Chandler

Available Now

RESTRAINING ORDER 1 & 2
By **CA$H & Coffee**

LOVE KNOWS NO BOUNDARIES 1-3
By **Coffee**

RAISED AS A GOON I, II, III & IV
BRED BY THE SLUMS I, II, III
BLAST FOR ME I & II
ROTTEN TO THE CORE I II III
A BRONX TALE I, II, III
DUFFLE BAG CARTEL I II III IV V VI
HEARTLESS GOON I II III IV V
A SAVAGE DOPEBOY I II
DRUG LORDS I II III
CUTTHROAT MAFIA I II
KING OF THE TRENCHES
By **Ghost**

LAY IT DOWN I & II
LAST OF A DYING BREED I II
BLOOD STAINS OF A SHOTTA I & II III
By **Jamaica**

LOYAL TO THE GAME I II III
LIFE OF SIN I, II III
By **TJ & Jelissa**

IF LOVING HIM IS WRONG…I & II
LOVE ME EVEN WHEN IT HURTS I II III
By **Jelissa**

CORNER BOY | COREY ROBINSON

BLOODY COMMAS I & II
SKI MASK CARTEL I, II & III
KING OF NEW YORK I II, III IV V
RISE TO POWER I II III
COKE KINGS I II III IV V
BORN HEARTLESS I II III IV
KING OF THE TRAP I II
By **T.J. Edwards**

WHEN THE STREETS CLAP BACK I & II III
THE HEART OF A SAVAGE I II III IV
MONEY MAFIA I II
LOYAL TO THE SOIL I II III
By **Jibril Williams**

A DISTINGUISHED THUG STOLE MY HEART I II &
III
LOVE SHOULDN'T HURT I II III IV
RENEGADE BOYS 1-4
PAID IN KARMA 1-3
SAVAGE STORMS 1-3
AN UNFORESEEN LOVE 1-3
BABY, I'M WINTERTIME COLD 1-3
A THUG'S STREET PRINCESS 1&2
By **Meesha**

A GANGSTER'S CODE 1-3
A GANGSTER'S SYN 1-3
THE SAVAGE LIFE 1-3
CHAINED TO THE STREETS 1-3
BLOOD ON THE MONEY 1-3
A GANGSTA'S PAIN 1-3
BEAUTIFUL LIES AND UGLY TRUTHS
CHURCH IN THESE STREETS
By **J-Blunt**

PUSH IT TO THE LIMIT
By **Bre' Hayes**

BLOOD OF A BOSS 1-5
SHADOWS OF THE GAME
TRAP BASTARD
By **Askari**

THE STREETS BLEED MURDER 1-3
THE HEART OF A GANGSTA 1-3
By **Jerry Jackson**

CUM FOR ME 1-8
An LDP Erotica Collaboration

BRIDE OF A HUSTLA 1-3
THE FETTI GIRLS 1-3
CORRUPTED BY A GANGSTA 1-4
BLINDED BY HIS LOVE
THE PRICE YOU PAY FOR LOVE 1-3
DOPE GIRL MAGIC 1-3
By **Destiny Skai**

WHEN A GOOD GIRL GOES BAD
By **Adrienne**

A KINGPIN'S AMBITION
A KINGPIN'S AMBITION II
I MURDER FOR THE DOUGH
By **Ambitious**

THE COST OF LOYALTY 1-3
By **Kweli**

CORNER BOY | COREY ROBINSON

A GANGSTER'S REVENGE 1-4
THE BOSS MAN'S DAUGHTERS 1-5
A SAVAGE LOVE 1&2
BAE BELONGS TO ME 1&2
A HUSTLER'S DECEIT 1-3
WHAT BAD BITCHES DO 1-3
SOUL OF A MONSTER 1-3
KILL ZONE
A DOPE BOY'S QUEEN 1-3
TIL DEATH 1-3
IMMA DIE BOUT MINE 1-3
By **Aryanna**

TRUE SAVAGE 1-7
DOPE BOY MAGIC 1-3
MIDNIGHT CARTEL 1-3
CITY OF KINGZ 1&2
NIGHTMARE ON SILENT AVE
THE PLUG OF LIL MEXICO 1&2
CLASSIC CITY
By **Chris Green**

A DOPEBOY'S PRAYER
By **Eddie "Wolf" Lee**

THE KING CARTEL 1-3
By **Frank Gresham**

THESE NIGGAS AIN'T LOYAL 1-3
By **Nikki Tee**

GANGSTA SHYT 1-3
By **CATO**

THE ULTIMATE BETRAYAL
By **Phoenix**

BOSS'N UP 1-3
By **Royal Nicole**

I LOVE YOU TO DEATH
By **Destiny J**

I RIDE FOR MY HITTA
I STILL RIDE FOR MY HITTA
By **Misty Holt**

LOVE & CHASIN' PAPER
By **Qay Crockett**

TO DIE IN VAIN
SINS OF A HUSTLA
By **ASAD**

BROOKLYN HUSTLAZ
By **Boogsy Morina**

BROOKLYN ON LOCK 1 & 2
By **Sonovia**

GANGSTA CITY
By **Teddy Duke**

A DRUG KING AND HIS DIAMOND 1-3
A DOPEMAN'S RICHES
HER MAN, MINE'S TOO 1&2
CASH MONEY HO'S
THE WIFEY I USED TO BE 1&2
PRETTY GIRLS DO NASTY THINGS
By **Nicole Goosby**

CORNER BOY | COREY ROBINSON

LIPSTICK KILLAH 1-3
CRIME OF PASSION 1-3
FRIEND OR FOE 1-3
By **Mimi**

TRAPHOUSE KING 1-3
KINGPIN KILLAZ 1-3
STREET KINGS 1&2
PAID IN BLOOD 1&2
CARTEL KILLAZ 1-3
DOPE GODS 1&2
By **Hood Rich**

STEADY MOBBN' 1-3
THE STREETS STAINED MY SOUL 1-3
By **Marcellus Allen**

WHO SHOT YA 1-3
SON OF A DOPE FIEND 1-3
HEAVEN GOT A GHETTO 1&2
SKI MASK MONEY 1&2
By **Renta**

GORILLAZ IN THE BAY 1-4
TEARS OF A GANGSTA 1/&2
3X KRAZY 1&2
STRAIGHT BEAST MODE 1&2
By **DE'KARI**

TRIGGADALE 1-3
MURDA WAS THE CASE 1-3
By **Elijah R. Freeman**

THE STREETS ARE CALLING
By **Duquie Wilson**

SLAUGHTER GANG 1-3
RUTHLESS HEART 1-3
By **Willie Slaughter**

GOD BLESS THE TRAPPERS 1-3
THESE SCANDALOUS STREETS 1-3
FEAR MY GANGSTA 1-5
THESE STREETS DON'T LOVE NOBODY 1-2
BURY ME A G 1-5
A GANGSTA'S EMPIRE 1-4
THE DOPEMAN'S BODYGAURD 1&2
THE REALEST KILLAZ 1-3
THE LAST OF THE OGS 1-3
By **Tranay Adams**

MARRIED TO A BOSS 1-3
By **Destiny Skai & Chris Green**

KINGZ OF THE GAME 1-7
CRIME BOSS 1-3
By **Playa Ray**

FUK SHYT
By **Blakk Diamond**

DON'T F#CK WITH MY HEART 1&2
By **Linnea**

ADDICTED TO THE DRAMA 1-3
IN THE ARM OF HIS BOSS
By **Jamila**

LOYALTY AIN'T PROMISED 1&2
By **Keith Williams**

CORNER BOY | COREY ROBINSON

YAYO 1-4
A SHOOTER'S AMBITION 1&2
BRED IN THE GAME
By **S. Allen**

TRAP GOD 1-3
RICH $AVAGE 1-3
MONEY IN THE GRAVE 1-3
CARTEL MONEY
By **Martell Troublesome Bolden**

FOREVER GANGSTA 1&2
GLOCKS ON SATIN SHEETS 1&2
By **Adrian Dulan**

TOE TAGZ 1-4
LEVELS TO THIS SHYT 1&2
IT'S JUST ME AND YOU
By **Ah'Million**

KINGPIN DREAMS 1-3
RAN OFF ON DA PLUG
By **Paper Boi Rari**

CONFESSIONS OF A GANGSTA 1-4
CONFESSIONS OF A JACKBOY 1-3
CONFESSIONS OF A HITMAN
By **Nicholas Lock**

I'M NOTHING WITHOUT HIS LOVE
SINS OF A THUG
TO THE THUG I LOVED BEFORE
A GANGSTA SAVED XMAS
IN A HUSTLER I TRUST
By **Monet Dragun**

QUIET MONEY 1-3
THUG LIFE 1-3
EXTENDED CLIP 1&2
A GANGSTA'S PARADISE
By **Trai'Quan**

CAUGHT UP IN THE LIFE 1-3
THE STREETS NEVER LET GO 1-3
By **Robert Baptiste**

NEW TO THE GAME 1-3
MONEY, MURDER & MEMORIES 1-3
By **Malik D. Rice**

CREAM 2-3
THE STREETS WILL TALK
By **Yolanda Moore**

LIFE OF A SAVAGE 1-4
A GANGSTA'S QUR'AN 1-4
MURDA SEASON 1-3
GANGLAND CARTEL 1-3
CHI'RAQ GANGSTAS 1-4
KILLERS ON ELM STREET 1-3
JACK BOYZ N DA BRONX 1-3
A DOPEBOY'S DREAM 1-3
JACK BOYS VS DOPE BOYS 1-3
COKE GIRLZ
COKE BOYS
SOSA GANG 1&2
BRONX SAVAGES
BODYMORE KINGPINS
BLOOD OF A GOON
By **Romell Tukes**

CORNER BOY | COREY ROBINSON

THE STREETS MADE ME 1-3
By **Larry D. Wright**

CONCRETE KILLA 1-3
VICIOUS LOYALTY 1-3
By **Kingpen**

THE ULTIMATE SACRIFICE 1-6
KHADIFI
IF YOU CROSS ME ONCE 1-3
ANGEL 1-4
IN THE BLINK OF AN EYE
By **Anthony Fields**

THE LIFE OF A HOOD STAR
By **Ca$h & Rashia Wilson**

THE STREETS WILL NEVER CLOSE 1-3
By **K'ajji**

NIGHTMARES OF A HUSTLA 1-3
By **King Dream**

HARD AND RUTHLESS 1&2
MOB TOWN 251
THE BILLIONAIRE BENTLEYS 1-3
REAL G'S MOVE IN SILENCE
By **Von Diesel**

GHOST MOB
By **Stilloan Robinson**

MOB TIES 1-6
SOUL OF A HUSTLER, HEART OF A KILLER 1-3
GORILLAZ IN THE TRENCHES
By **SayNoMore**

BODYMORE MURDERLAND 1-3
THE BIRTH OF A GANGSTER 1-4
By **Delmont Player**

FOR THE LOVE OF A BOSS 1&2
By **C. D. Blue**

KILLA KOUNTY 1-5
By **Khufu**

MOBBED UP 1-4
THE BRICK MAN 1-5
THE COCAINE PRINCESS 1-10
STEPPERS 1-3
SUPER GREMLIN 1-4
By **King Rio**

MONEY GAME 1&2
By **Smoove Dolla**

A GANGSTA'S KARMA 1-4
By **FLAME**

KING OF THE TRENCHES 1-3
By **GHOST & TRANAY ADAMS**

QUEEN OF THE ZOO 1&2
By **Black Migo**

GRIMEY WAYS 1-3
By **Ray Vinci**

XMAS WITH AN ATL SHOOTER
By **Ca$h & Destiny Skai**

CORNER BOY | COREY ROBINSON

KING KILLA 1&2
By **Vincent "Vitto" Holloway**

BETRAYAL OF A THUG 1&2
By **Fre$h**

THE MURDER QUEENS 1-5
By **Michael Gallon**

FOR THE LOVE OF BLOOD 1-4
By **Jamel Mitchell**

HOOD CONSIGLIERE 1&2
NO TIME FOR ERROR
By **Keese**

PROTÉGÉ OF A LEGEND 1&2
LOVE IN THE TRENCHES 1&2
By **Corey Robinson**

BORN IN THE GRAVE 1-3
CRIME PAYS
By **Self Made Tay**

MOAN IN MY MOUTH
By **XTASY**

TORN BETWEEN A GANGSTER AND A GENTLEMAN
By **J-BLUNT & Miss Kim**

LOYALTY IS EVERYTHING 1-3
CITY OF SMOKE 1&2
By **Molotti**

HERE TODAY GONE TOMORROW 1&2
By **Fly Rock**

WOMEN LIE MEN LIE 1-4
FIFTY SHADES OF SNOW 1-3
STACK BEFORE YOU SPLURGE
GIRLS FALL LIKE DOMINOES
NAÏVE TO THE STREETS
By **ROY MILLIGAN**

PILLOW PRINCESS
By **S. Hawkins**

THE BUTTERFLY MAFIA 1-3
SALUTE MY SAVAGERY 1&2
By **Fumiya Payne**

THE LANE 1&2
By Ken-Ken Spence

THE PUSSY TRAP 1-5
By **Nene Capri**

DIRTY DNA
By **Blaque**

SANCTIFIED AND HORNY
by **XTASY**

BOOKS BY LDP'S CEO, CA$H

TRUST IN NO MAN
TRUST IN NO MAN 2
TRUST IN NO MAN 3
BONDED BY BLOOD
SHORTY GOT A THUG
THUGS CRY
THUGS CRY 2
THUGS CRY 3
TRUST NO BITCH
TRUST NO BITCH 2
TRUST NO BITCH 3
TIL MY CASKET DROPS
RESTRAINING ORDER
RESTRAINING ORDER 2
IN LOVE WITH A CONVICT
LIFE OF A HOOD STAR
XMAS WITH AN ATL SHOOTER

www.ingramcontent.com/pod-product-compliance
Lightning Source LLC
Chambersburg PA
CBHW070512260626
47161CB00004B/1529